MW00639859

MONTANA GUARDIAN

A GUARDIAN SECURITY NOVELLA

KRIS MICHAELS

WWW.KRISMICHAELSAUTHOR.COM

Copyright © 2018 by Kris Michaels

All rights reserved.

No part of this book may be reproduced in any form or by any electronic or mechanical means, including information storage and retrieval systems, without written permission from the author, except for the use of brief quotations in a book review.

Licensed material is being used for illustrative purposes only and any person depicted int the licensed material is a model. This book is fiction. Names, characters, some locations and incidents are the product of the author's imagination or used fictionally. Any resemblance to actual person, living or dead, events, or locations are entirely coincidental.

❃ Created with Vellum

INTRODUCTION

Dearest Reader,

This is small glimpse into Sierra Team, who you met in Justin's book. Other team members and characters depicted in The Kings of Guardian and Guardian Shadow World will have their own stories. Will they be full length novels or novellas? I never know until the characters speak.

Thank you for supporting me. I adore each and every one of you.

Hugs,

Kris

CHAPTER 1

*V*an Wheeler's phone pinged and the screen lit.

>**Call in: 1545hrs. Report to Andrews AFB:1800hrs**

"Yo! Travis." As he read the text message from his Guardian handler, Van Wheeler called to his teammate, Travis Coleman.

"What's up, Skipper?"

He grinned and lobbed his phone at his long-time friend. "Pack your bags, we're heading out."

Travis caught the phone and read the text. "I'll tell the team." Van's phone flew back on an errant trajectory. "Wonder what the op is this time."

Van lurched and snatched the device from the air at the last minute, saving the framed picture of his family on the wall behind him. "You sure as fuck can't throw."

"Not a job requirement." Travis answered while texting.

"Right, ever heard of hand grenades?" The corner of his mouth quirked as Travis lifted a middle finger. They'd met while surviving boot camp at Paris Island and then had gone their own way through follow-on training. He'd lost track of his best friend until they'd landed in the same Marine Corps Forces Special Operations Command unit and remained MARSOC team members through years of combat. Guardian approached Van when he started searching for a job at the end of his enlistment. He interviewed, and when his Guardian interviewer asked if he knew of any other candidates for the open positions, he recommended Travis. The rest, as they say, was history.

Guardian Security held the position of the world's preeminent private security agency and one with global reach. As such, federal agencies and private concerns in the United States, as well as foreign interests and nations around the world, employed their elite services. Guardian's missions dealt with everything from computer security breaches to privately funded military operations in hostile areas. Van's team specialized in the latter.

Since his promotion to Skipper of Sierra team, he'd learned to roll with the assignments. Weeks, or even months, could stretch between missions, so Sierra team spent downtime at one of Guardian's stateside facilities, honing weapons and tactical skills and learning intel on what the bastards overseas were throwing at the teams deployed to hostile areas. Until an overseas assignment surfaced, Sierra team performed duty in the States as a backup force for domestic issues. Whatever the op was, it had to be important...or required one of his team's specialized skills. His team had just transitioned off their most recent overseas rotation in Syria and had barely cleared their mandatory downtime.

The time displayed on the face of his phone indicated five minutes until he needed to call in for his mission brief.

"Shit, that means I need to go close up my apartment," Travis mused as he wandered into the Van's kitchen. The telltale sound of the refrigerator opening meant his XO was eating again.

Van padded barefoot down the hall of his apartment. Other than his toiletries, his go-bag was packed. He tossed a bar of soap, shampoo, deodorant, toothpaste, a toothbrush, and a comb, into a worn leather carrier. He was ready to deploy.

"Heading out, Skipper. Ricco, Scuba and Harley have acknowledged notification."

"Rally point?" Van asked as he entered the front room of his apartment.

"Here, of course. You have *food*," Travis shouted as he let himself out of the apartment.

Van huffed a laugh. It was true. He'd just spent two hundred dollars on groceries. He wasn't worried. His team would eat through whatever he had in the apartment before they left on Guardian's latest assignment. Van sprawled onto the sofa and grabbed his phone. He tapped in the numbers to the switchboard.

"Operator Two-Five-Three."

Van could swear that woman's voice was a recording, but her greeting always varied, so unless Guardian had implemented one hell of an Artificial Intelligence program... "Commander, Sierra Team."

"Good Afternoon, Skipper. One moment, I'll connect you with Domestic Operations."

Van had no idea how the woman knew where

to direct the calls. He never asked to be transferred to a person. She just automatically knew what to do. Freaky, in a *Twilight Zone* kinda way.

"Good afternoon, Skipper."

A soft female voice he didn't recognize surprised him. "Ah...good afternoon?"

"Standby for the Ops O." Her voice once again floated across the connection.

Well, that would be beneficial. Kannon Starling was the Operations Officer for the Washington D.C. District Manager. He and his scheduler, Willa, were miracle workers who kept the teams rotating and provided them all with mandatory downtime. The sultry velvet voice on the line wasn't Willa because Willa sounded like she'd smoked cigarettes for eighty years and still had one dangling out of her mouth.

"Wheeler? Starling here. Standby while we verify the line is secure."

Van immediately recognized the Ops O's voice. "Roger that, sir."

"The line is secure." The woman's voice floated to him once again.

"Authenticate Bulldog." Starling's brash burst of words assaulted his ears like sandpaper after the caress of the female voice.

He responded with his countersign. "Chesty, sir." Chesty Puller was one bulldog of a mother-fucker and one of the best damn generals the Marine Corps ever produced.

"Jewell King is on the line. She runs computer security for Guardian." Starling spit the words out in rapid-fire succession.

"Roger, sir. I know who she is." Every Guardian employee knew of the Kings of Guardian. That family ran the multi-billion-dollar company.

The woman chuckled before she spoke. "Skipper, I have a unique mission for you. For reasons I can't go into right now, I need you and one of your team members to head to Buckskin Junction.

Starling came on the line just as Van opened his mouth to ask questions.

"Two people only, Wheeler. You pick who goes with you. The other three will be utilized in a joint operation we are working with Homeland. You know we wouldn't split you up unless we were pushed. We're being pushed hard."

"Roger that, sir. I'll take Travis."

"You have knowledge of the area, correct?"

"Limited knowledge, at best."

Jewell King's question surprised him. It shouldn't have. He'd heard rumors of the woman's research skills. Seems like the rumors were true. He *was* somewhat familiar with the region. His grandfather had owned a ranch west of Wisdom, Montana. He'd visited it when he was a child through his teen years until his grandfather died and his dad sold the old ranch.

"Affirmative and understood. One of our specialists is a freelancer, and she resides in the area. She's off the grid and has been for the last year. Since you worked with her during her last operation with us, we'd like you to make contact."

Van closed his eyes and shook his head. Fuck, it couldn't be. *Don't say it...don't say it...don't let it be her...for the love of God...*

Starling confirmed his apprehension. "We need you to locate Cassie Valentine and tell her we have an assignment for her."

Son of a bitch. "Sir, with all due respect, I think you should find someone else to do this mission."

"You're joking, right? I just told you I'm so fucking swamped with shit coming down the pipe that I'm busting up your team to cover the cesspool I'm swimming in. Unless you have a damn good reason, you and Travis get your asses to Andrews. We have a Guardian jet inbound. They are refueling and then turning and burning.

Wheels up at 1900hrs." Starling's gruff voice left little room for argument.

"Roger that, sir. Wheels up at 1900hrs," Van replied calmly as his mind spewed every cuss word in every language he'd ever learned.

"Get in, get the message to her, get out, and call in for further instructions."

"Roger that, sir."

Jewell chimed in with additional information. "We have two points of contact in the area that can assist you in locating her. The first is the local sheriff, Casey Black. The second is a local contractor who has worked with Guardian in the past. He's a specialist. His name is Isiah Reichs. He's a former Marine. He's a man we can trust. He has contacts and knows the local area. I'll have Domestic Operations call and make contact with both men to let them know you're on your way. I've also sent their contact information to your phone." He could hear the distinct sound of a keyboard in the background as she spoke. "Commander, I cannot stress how important it is that we find Cassie Valentine. When you locate her, you are to give her the following message, 'The puzzle master is necessary.'"

Van took a deep breath before he acknowledged his mission. "Roger, I copy. 'The puzzle master is necessary.'" *Why in the hell didn't Guardian just ask the local contractor to do this mission. What the hell was his name...Reichs, that was it.*

"I'll also need you to escort her in, if necessary. I'm not sure of her status, but you may be required to arrange her travel and bring her in, that's why we aren't asking Reichs to deliver the message. He's obligated to another operation and must be ready to leave at a moment's notice."

Perfect, and that scrubs that argument. "We'll find her, relay the message and get her to you if necessary." Van parroted the directives he'd been given.

In the tag team phone call, the next voice he heard was Starling. "Tell Ricco to call in. I'll give him reporting instructions for the rest of the team." Abruptly, the call disconnected.

Van looked at the blank face of his cell, dropped it on the coffee table and stood, running his hands through his hair in frustration. *Cassie Valentine.* Fuck him standing. What in the fuck had he done to deserve this seventh level of hell?

He grabbed his phone to give Travis the plan. His team wasn't going to like it, but Guardian was the best at what they did, so no one was going to question the directives. No one except him. *Cassie fucking Valentine*. All those curves, blonde hair, and dark brown eyes. She had a smile so warm and inviting it could melt the polar ice caps. And her body…Van dropped the thought like a piece of burning metal. There was no way he was going to start questioning what the fuck had gone wrong… again. No, he had a call to make, and his once-upon-a-time relationship with the best code breaker in the free world wasn't something he wanted to revisit.

He opened his phone and hit up Travis. His XO could contact the rest of his team.

"Yo." Travis's answer was short and succinct.

"Tell Ricco, Scuba, and Harley they aren't coming with us. I'll brief you on the mission when you get here. Ricco needs to call the switchboard. Ops O has orders for the three of them." The distinct absence of comments told him just how confused his XO was feeling. Well, join the club.

"Van, man…did we fuck up somehow?" Travis used his first name instead of calling him Skipper. Yeah, his XO was concerned.

"No, we're good. Ops O is hard pressed and needs to use his assets wisely. Call the team. Let them know this isn't permanent."

"Roger that. I'll be back at yours in twenty."

Van acknowledged the comment and tossed the phone down again. He dropped to the couch and closed his eyes, wondering why in the hell he was selected for this assignment. Fate was a bitch sometimes, but right now he had a few choice names for fate, and they weren't near as nice as bitch. Over a year ago his team, along with Ms. Valentine, had traveled into Kashmir and set up a listening post to gather intelligence on the Hizbul Mujahideen. Ms. Valentine accompanied them because she was the best code breaker available. Previous teams, partnered with some of the best linguistic specialists in the world, had failed to understand the gibberish the HM was transmitting.

His team met up with Cassie in Denver and made their way to Kashmir through covert channels. She'd been waiting for them at a truck stop at the edge of the city. She stood quietly beside a solid, older man. After they introduced themselves, the man pulled her aside to have a word with her. Van got the impression the comments weren't well wishes.

Cassie never looked the older man in the face, her gaze pinned to the ground. The man shook her arm, and Cassie nodded while holding herself at a distance...as if she was afraid he'd strike her. As a unit, his team stepped forward. The only way that conversation would continue was if the man took his fucking hands off her. Van remembered the moment he plucked the man's fingers off of Cassie.

"Get your hands off me," the older man snarled his comments at Van.

"Nobody touches a lady like that." Van stepped closer and tightened his grip.

The man flexed the muscles of his forearm and tried to pull away, successful only when Van loosened his grip. "Get her back on the day you promised. Not one day later." He spun on his heel and made his way to an old rusted out truck with Montana plates.

"Are you alright?" Ricco, the medic in the group, asked as Van and Travis formed a human shield between the woman and the asshole getting into the truck.

"Thank you. I'm fine. It doesn't hurt." She rubbed her arm where the guy's meat hooks had latched onto her.

Ricco took her hand in his and pushed up the sleeve of her thermal shirt. The elastic was worn, so there was little resistance, and that was when Van turned and saw the kaleidoscope of purple, green and yellow bruises blotting her arm and elbow.

"Did he do that to you?" Van ground out. If he did, the fucker's days were numbered. Harley, Travis, and Scuba made themselves scarce, and the woman seemed to relax.

"No. I fell." She pulled her arm back and shoved her sleeve down.

"Right, okay. Who was that?"

Ricco picked up the woman's bag and left Van alone with her.

"My uncle." She glanced at where the truck had been parked and then searched the parking lot.

"Why is he so particular about you being back on a certain date?" Van motioned toward where his team had moved. He wanted to give her the choice of following or not.

"Ah...my mom's not well. I need to make sure I get back to her." She started towards the two Suburbans where his team was now gathered.

"As it stands right now, we're scheduled to be back in country three days before he wants you back." That date was almost three months in the future. Anything could happen between now and then, so Van cautioned her. "The return date isn't a guarantee. It's always fluid. Have you told Guardian that you need to be back stateside by a specific date?" Van didn't want to be the reason that bastard put his hands on the woman again.

She nodded her head and whispered, "Guardian knows about the date."

The trip overseas was uneventful. They got in and set up a listening post. It seemed the further away from Denver they got, the more Cassie came to life, like a flower opening before their eyes. Within four days of pitching their tents, Cassie had broken the code the bastards had developed. The six of them worked in eight-hour shifts monitoring and decoding the transmissions using the cipher Cassie had developed.

Van and Cassie worked together during the day shift. They ate together and slept within a few feet of each other for weeks. She was kind, giving, innocent and trusting. Her wide-eyed wonder at just about everything made him realize how jaded he'd become and how vulnerable and sheltered she was. She blushed at the most ordinary kindness and was unusually timid. Her behavior suggested that bastard uncle of hers abused her. That thought sent his blood into a boil. How anyone could abuse such a beautiful soul baffled him. Cassie shrugged off his questions about her family, telling him only that her father and uncle were religious and very strict.

Cassie's unwavering kindness never faltered,

even under less than desirable field conditions. She always made sure his men had enough to eat before she would take any food. She collected dirty clothes and washed them, even when they insisted she didn't have to clean after them. Her hands never stilled, and her sweet, honest interactions with his men melted the toughened warriors. Everyone adored the quiet, shy woman.

Working in close quarters, he and Cassie managed to resist the attraction they felt for each other. Until they didn't. Was it a huge fuck-up on his part? *Hell yes.* Unprofessional, undisciplined and against every ethics standard he'd sworn to uphold. He didn't care. The simple, beautiful woman was *it* for him.

Another team relieved them, and Sierra team traveled back to the States—where Cassie fucking disappeared without so much as a word. When they arrived in Atlanta, he'd told her he'd meet her in the hotel lobby at six. She never showed. He called Guardian, and the only answer he received was that her contract was over. Due to her electives on her contract, her personal information couldn't be given out without written permission. A fucking Catch-22 situation. He couldn't get her information without written permission, but he couldn't get written permission without her personal information. He felt like his face had been used as a jackhammer against the largest fucking brick wall in Atlanta. No matter what favors he called in or what strings he pulled, he couldn't get her contact information.

Van sucked air in and pushed it out, counting to three between each action. The woman had played him. Hard. He'd never seen deceit in her eyes, had never seen the thoughtlessness and coldness of heart it had to have taken just to say, 'Fuck you,' and walk away. Hell, the woman hadn't even given him the courtesy of those two words. He scrubbed his face and leaned forward. Besides the friendship they'd developed, he *knew* they'd clicked...and in a special way. They fit together in a fashion he'd never experienced before, and he absolutely knew Cassie Valentine was the woman he could have spent the remainder of his life loving.

I'm so fucked. Cassie. He turned to look out the window. His superiors had put his back against a stone wall. He *had* to go. The woman had gutted him, and it had taken the last year for him to deal with the way she'd just walked away. He shook his head again. Fuck, he really thought they had something. Obviously, Cassie didn't feel the same way. He wiped his chin with a hand, ruffling his beard before he combed it back down. He had no choice. He would do what he was instructed because he was loyal and a damn good team leader. He'd find Cassie, relay the message, bring her in—and not one damn thing more.

J ewell King disconnected Van Wheeler from the three-way call.

Kannon Starling immediately growled over the phone, "You better know what you're doing."

Starling's grandstanding didn't faze her. She had five brothers and an ex-assassin for a husband, all of whom could growl and snarl far more effectively than the Ops O. "I do know what I'm doing. I believe you know I have the authority to reroute assets as necessary to ensure operations underway are not impeded or exposed."

"Emergency protocols, yeah, I get it, but I don't see an emergency here. I don't like it. Splitting that team up was wrong. I don't like not knowing what the mission is. My clearance is high enough. You need to feed me some information or I'll go to Alpha."

"My clearance is higher than Alpha's, and he hasn't been read into this op. You *could* go to Archangel and demand the information." Jewell smirked at her hands-free device. She had him over a barrel.

"Get my men back to me ASAP," Starling groused before he cut the connection.

Jewell leaned back in her huge leather chair and pulled her feet up, wrapping her arms around her legs, leaning her chin on her knees. There was no way the man would go over her head to her brother Jason. Nobody wanted to deal with Archangel.

She scanned the code that rolled up her computer screen. Her programs hadn't been able to crack it. A shit storm was brewing. If Starling did go to one of her brothers to demand answers, she had enough information to justify her actions. Her gut told her the messages she'd stumbled across on the dark net were dangerous. She just couldn't prove it. Yet. Guardian needed Cassie Valentine. There was no one better at what she did.

CHAPTER 2

an maneuvered the vehicle out of Wisdom and found the road to Buckskin Junction without the aid of the GPS. There had been some growth in the hamlet of Wisdom, but not much. Once they got on the road, his mind drifted back in time. He could barely remember the town of Buckskin Junction, but he did remember driving up to Butte to the hardware store with his grandfather. It didn't matter what they went to buy, a brown paper bag filled with nails, a new ax head, or even a broom, his grandfather would let him carry the treasure to the truck before they would head home and go to the one and only diner in Buckskin Junction. One of his most vivid memories of the small town was the banana cream pie his grandfather would order. They would always split it. Damn, his mouth watered at the memory.

"We are not in Kansas anymore, Toto." Travis spoke low as he gazed out the window to the west. The Bitterroot Mountains were majestic. Van remembered that sense of awe, too. He would sit and stare at the mountain range from his grandfather's porch during the long summers of his childhood.

The small town came into view, and he decelerated. The land that time forgot. His hazy memories sharpened as the dusty streets and vintage buildings fired long forgotten memories. He turned off the interstate and followed the directions on his GPS to the sheriff's substation. Not that it was difficult to find. A marked county sheriff's car was parked out front. He'd been instructed to check in with the local law enforcement before he met up with Isiah Reichs at the Stirrup. It was a dive at the edge of the small settlement that had been there as long as Van could remember. He glanced at his watch. His meeting with Reichs was set for eight, and it was just now six.

He pulled up behind the marked cars and cut off his engine. He and Travis got out of the

Guardian SUV and stretched. They'd been traveling for the last twenty-four hours. They departed on time last night, landed in South Dakota, and after meeting with Guardian personnel at the training complex at the base of the Black Hills, they drove to their destination in Montana. They took US 212 to Interstate 90 and soaked in all the vastness that South Dakota, Wyoming, and Montana. The grandeur of the vistas was enough to make a person feel small and insignificant.

He opened the door to the sheriff's office and walked in, leaving Travis to stare at the mountains.

"Hey, can I help you?" A deputy looked up from behind the desk where he sat. The old computer in front of him cast a bluish-green glow. Van glanced up at the unlit strips of fluorescent bulbs.

"Forget to pay your electric bill?"

The deputy leaned back in his chair. "Computer still has power."

Van laughed, not wanting to cross swords with the local officials. "So it does."

"The fluorescent lights give me one hell of a headache." He leaned forward and stared at Van before he glanced out the glass door and took a look at Travis. "What can I do for you?"

"My people called Sheriff Black yesterday. The name is Wheeler, I'm with Guardian Security."

"That so? We had a family of Wheelers who lived over in the next valley. Had a big ole ranch before the family sold it. Those real estate developer types chopped it up and built designer ranches."

Van nodded. "That would have been my grandfather's land. My father sold it after he passed."

"Well, I'll be damned. Small world. How did a country boy like you end up working for a hoity-toity organization like Guardian?"

Van laughed. He'd heard Guardian called many things, but hoity-toity was a new one. "I hired on with them when I got out of the Marine Corps. Is the sheriff around?"

"Nope. He had to go up to Butte. He meets up with all the local law enforcement representatives about once every other month, weather permitting. You know, troopers, municipal cops, and the like? If you ask me, it's a great way to get up there and eat at a fancy restaurant. Not too many excuses to do that. Anyway, he'll be back to work tomorrow morning. I can call him if necessary."

Van glanced over his shoulder as Travis walked in before he turned back to the deputy. "Could you leave a note for the sheriff and tell him we're in town. I've got a meeting with Isiah Reichs tonight to see if we can get a lead on a woman we are trying to connect with."

"Yeah, who is that? I know just about everyone in these parts." The deputy picked up a cellophane-wrapped toothpick and stripped the cover off before he popped it into the side of his mouth.

"Cassie Valentine." Travis volunteered the name and extended his hand. "Travis Coleman."

The deputy stood and shook Travis's hand. "Never heard of her. You sure you got the right neck of the woods?"

"Our information comes from a very reliable source. Thank you for your time, Deputy."

"You headed back to Butte tonight?"

"Nope, staying at the bed and breakfast." Van tapped the counter twice and threw the deputy a two-finger salute as they left the building.

Travis stopped and looked toward the west again. "Skipper, that is one beautiful view. Why on earth did you let your old man sell your grandpa's ranch?"

"Like I had any choice. Hell, I was fifteen. My old man hates the country. He's city, through and through. Besides, I wouldn't have had a clue how to manage the land or livestock properly."

Van turned the SUV around and drove the short distance to the diner. The place hadn't changed. Even the paint color was the same.

"Food any good?" Travis asked as he got out of the vehicle.

"Used be. Can't vouch for it now, but I need to eat something that doesn't come from a gas station."

"Hey, those pickled eggs and hot dogs were good." Travis slugged his arm and ducked away when Van punched him back.

"Dude, nobody eats that crap. You have no idea how long that shit had been rolling around on that warmer, and I swear, pickled eggs? How can you eat that shit?" Van opened the door and the rich, warm smell of home cooking immediately assaulted him.

They found a vacant booth toward the back and slid in. A harried waitress hustled to their table.

"Hi, my name is Mavis, and I'll be your server." She lifted an order pad and pulled a pen out from behind her ear. "What can I get you to drink?"

"Ice water and a cup of coffee, please." Travis

picked up the menu that Mavis had slapped down on the table.

"Make that two." Van echoed the order. The waitress gave them a quick smile and exited stage left. He searched the clientele. Several older couples occupied adjoining tables and he wondered if they might have known his grandfather. His father had left as soon as he'd graduated high school, and he'd never returned. Hell, he hadn't even flown with Van when he sent Van to his grandfather's every summer. At the age of six, he'd negotiated the flight and gate attendants that shuffled him from point A to point B on his own.

"So, Skipper, when are we going to talk about the elephant in the room?"

Van swung his attention back to Travis and slowly lifted one eyebrow, daring his friend to continue that line of thought.

"No, seriously. Cassie left you high and dry with no reason or explanation."

Travis shook his head, and Van took the opportunity to stop the conversation. "Thank you, Captain Obvious. I don't want to talk about it."

"How can we not talk about it? I mean, we are here to go fetch her out of whatever off-the-grid commune she's living in. It isn't like you two aren't going to meet when we give her the message, and from the sounds of it, she could be traveling with us if she accepts the assignment. Just saying...the elephant is pretty fucking big and sooner or later you two will have to talk. I'll make myself scarce when it does, but damn it, Van, she's got a lot to explain."

Mavis appeared with their drinks. "Ready to order?" She pulled some individual creamers and sugar packets out of her apron and piled them at the center of the table.

Travis gave her one of his 100-watt smiles before he asked, "What do you recommend?"

Mavis laughed turning several heads their direction. "Honey, this isn't a five-star restaurant. Everything here is good, solid food. The pies are fantastic."

"Okay, well then I'll have..." Travis opened the menu, closed his eyes, and pointed. When he opened his eyes, he laughed. "Guess I'll have the patty melt, fries, and a chocolate shake, please."

Mavis gave him a smile, scribbled on her pad and looked at Van.

"Chicken and dumplings and banana cream pie for dessert."

"Alright, I'll put this in." She spun on her heel and darted away from the table again.

"I didn't forget what we were talking about." Travis leaned back in the booth. "I've spent the last year putting you back together. She doesn't get to break you again."

He gave a burst of humorless laughter. "She didn't break me."

"Oh no? When was the last time you went out with the team? The last time you did anything besides train and hole up in your apartment? When were you last on a date?" Travis lifted his fingers as he spoke as if ticking items off a list. "When was the last time you thought of any other woman?"

Van held Travis's stare for several long seconds. He couldn't dispute a damn thing Travis had said. He *had* retreated into himself. Fuck, when you think you've met 'the one' and she leaves without a backward glance, you tend to become introspective. He'd searched his mind for any clue, any indication Cassie hadn't felt the same way he did. Granted, they hadn't said the words, but he'd shown her he loved her. Hell, he'd wanted to wait until they got back to the States to tell her, so he could treat her the way she deserved to be treated. Wine, dinner, dancing, and a proposal. Fuck, he wanted to do right by her, and all the while she was plotting her stealth mode escape. That did a number on a man's confidence. So, no, he hadn't gotten back on the horse. He didn't want a hook-up; besides, he had his right hand for relief.

What he wanted were answers. He ground his teeth together. He'd be damned if he'd ask. He didn't want to put himself on the line to be torn to shreds—again. That woman had stomped the fuck out of his heart. He wasn't going to give her the pieces he'd managed to cobble together. Van leaned back in the booth and chucked a creamer at Travis. "Drop it. We are doing this mission and getting the fuck out of Dodge. Professional, quick, and it is over."

"Good luck with that." Travis threw the creamer back at him.

The little plastic tub went ninety degrees to the right and Van had to lean into the aisle to catch it. He sat up and lifted the foil top, plopping the liquid into his coffee. "Man, I thank God you never had to use a hand grenade when we were in the military."

"Damn, that hurts, Skipper." Travis grabbed his chest and winced.

Mavis brought their food out and plunked the huge platters in front of them.

"You need anything else, just let me know." She didn't wait around for any commentary but hustled back to the kitchen window loading her arms down with plates.

"God, this looks amazing." Travis reached for the ketchup and squeezed a huge pool onto his plate. "Breakfast here?"

Van shrugged, "After I run. Sitting all day sucked." He lifted a spoonful of fluffy dumplings and chicken. An explosion of flavor in his mouth forced an almost orgasmic eye roll. Damn, maybe he'd double the run and take a lunch to go.

They managed to eat everything on their plates and Travis added to his order with a piece of apple pie and homemade vanilla ice cream. The banana cream pie was everything Van remembered. He hadn't realized how much he missed this place.

Travis stretched as they exited the diner. They'd both left Mavis one hell of a tip. The entire time they were in the establishment the woman never slowed down. She had to have walked a half marathon while they were eating.

"The Stirrup is over there." He pointed to the old house off the street and about two blocks away.

"That's where we'll meet Reichs. Let's get our bags stowed and head over. We can nurse a cold one while we wait for him."

Van let his eyes adjust to the dim interior before he and Travis made their way to the bar. A big guy ambled over and tossed two coasters in front of them.

"Howdy. Name's Melvin." The man extended his hand and he took it.

"Van, this is Travis."

The guy's grip was intense, so Van met power with power, earning him a slight nod when the handshake ended. He couldn't help but notice the bartender played the same game with Travis. His XO's grip tightened to the point where Melvin shook his hand out when they finished.

"What can I get you two?"

"I'll have whatever's on tap." Travis reached for a small bowl of nuts and pulled them toward him.

"The same." He shook his head. "Dammit, man, we just finished eating."

"Dude, that was like…fifteen minutes ago. It's already settled."

Melvin set the tall frosty mugs of beer in front of them. "You two just passing through?"

"Looking to meet up with someone." Van took a drink of the ice-cold beer after he answered the bartender.

"Yeah? Who would that be?"

"Isiah Reichs." Travis offered.

"Really? So, I'm guessing you've never met him?"

"Nope. Supposed to meet up with him here in about ten minutes."

Melvin braced his large arms on the bar and nodded toward the round booth along the back corner of the wall. "That would be him, the one wearing the blue shirt."

He turned on his stool and glanced the direction the bartender had indicated. Grabbing his beer, he motioned to Travis and tossed Melvin a "thank you" over his shoulder. He made his way to the booth, interrupting a conversation between the occupants.

"Isiah Reichs? I'm Van Wheeler and this is Travis Coleman.

The man stood and extended his hand. "Good to meet you. I must say I was surprised when Guardian made contact last night. I haven't heard from them in a while. Not that I'm opposed, but I'm happy keeping my head down and my ass from being shot."

Reichs indicated the bench seat, and he and Travis slid in across from Reichs. "From what my handlers tell me, you're squared away and have one hell of a reputation."

"I'd like to think so." Isiah nodded to his left and right. "This is Sampson Waters and my brother, Josiah. They work with me on my spread."

He nodded, noting the distinct military vibe each man put out, and returned his attention to Reichs. "We are looking for a woman who lives off the grid in the local area. Her name is Cassie Valentine."

Isiah cocked his head and leaned back in the booth. "I know of the Valentines. Getting up where they live isn't going to be easy, and from what I understand, they don't like unexpected company."

"They?" Travis grabbed a handful of popcorn out of a large bowl on the table.

Van rolled his eyes at his bottomless pit of an XO.

"That's an assumption. I got the impression it was a family up there. I've never met them. I'm basing this information on a conversation I had with a ranger…oh, hell, it had to be a couple years back. He works the area west of here. From what I recall, they own a small plot of land smack in the middle of the Bitterroot Mountains."

"Why would anyone want to live way up there?" Travis managed to ask the question between mouthfuls of popcorn.

"Gold. There are still some miners up there. Few and far between, but if they are up there, they've probably been bitten by gold fever." Reichs took another drink of his beer and cocked his head, watching Travis demolish the bowl of popcorn.

"Can you get us in contact with that ranger?" Van couldn't imagine Cassie living hard. Well, he could, but he sure as hell didn't want to picture it. She deserved to be pampered and cared for…. No, he wasn't going to go there. He couldn't. This was a mission and nothing more.

"Let me see if I can track him down. May I ask why you need to find Ms. Valentine?" Isiah took a drink of his beer. "I need to know what I'm getting into."

"Sir, if I knew, I'd tell you. What I do know is that Cassie, like yourself, is a freelancer for

Guardian and they have sent us here to find her and give her a message."

"That's one hell of a lot of trouble to go to for a message," Sampson spoke, bringing all eyes to him. "I've ridden up in those mountains, hell, we all have. Getting back that far will take a couple days and some damn good trail horses."

Van palmed the back of his neck and rubbed. "I'll call Guardian and start them acquiring the equipment we'll need."

"You won't be making that call. Lucky for you, I know a man." Isiah Reichs lifted his glass and emptied the remainder of his drink. "I have the horses you'll need and the gear to camp up at that elevation. Let's meet up tomorrow morning, 0800hrs at my place, the Tangled Root Ranch. That way." Reichs pointed his finger. Van took note of the direction. "You'll see the turn-off. It's marked."

"Roger that, sir. Thank you for the assist."

"Not a problem. Besides, someday I might need a hand from Guardian. I hear the teams these days have all the good toys."

"Yes, sir. Only the best." Which was the truth. Guardian never let their teams go into the field without the latest tech and weaponry.

Isiah nodded, finished his drink and stood up,

ending the meeting. "Do you have a place to stay tonight?"

"Yes sir, we are over at the bed and breakfast." Van stood and shook the man's hand again along with his brother and Waters. He knew all three men were prior military. It was something ingrained in a person, and it was easy to recognize one of your own.

"Alright. See you in the morning." Reichs waved at Melvin behind the bar, and all three men made their way out of the bar.

Van motioned toward the door, and Travis got up slowly, snagging the last of the popcorn before he followed him out.

"Things just got a little more interesting. Reichs never did say how many he thought were up there. Does she have family up there with her?"

Van shrugged. He knew of her mom, dad, and uncle. He wasn't going to torture himself with the idea that Cassie had a significant other. Everything he knew about the woman led him to believe she would never cheat on whomever she wound up loving—even if it wasn't him. He shook off the thought and answered his friend, "I don't have a fucking clue. We'll play it by ear, but I think we need to tread lightly. Reichs doesn't have firsthand knowledge of what is going on up there. We'll consider her home turf as hostile until we know different. In the morning, once we get the general location from Reichs, I'll call Operations and get a satellite sweep of the area. At least we'll have an accurate bird's-eye view of the terrain."

"Roger that." Travis cleared his throat like he did when he was nervous. "You know something you might need to consider, Skipper…she could be married."

"Can't say I haven't thought about that." Hell, there was not a scenario he hadn't considered.

CHAPTER 3

*H*e tossed and turned on the too-soft mattress and flipped the covers off. The steam radiators were cranked to the max, and the window was either painted or nailed shut. Either way, he felt like he was in a sauna. He glanced at his watch again. Three minutes later than when he'd last checked. He lifted off the bed as quietly as he could and tried the window again, this time using his utility knife to separate the painted sash from the window sill. Halle-fucking-lujah! The window opened, and fresh air poured into the room. Van folded his knife and placed it beside his .45 on the bedside table. He lowered himself back onto the bed and prayed for silence. As if. The bed creaked with each movement he made. The old brass bed looked great in the room but sleeping on the floor was becoming an attractive alternative.

Van turned his head and gazed out the window at the full moon that illuminated the night sky. Vivid memories of another full moon, half the world away, invaded his thoughts. The first night he and Cassie made love, the moon was full and so damn close. A harvest moon, that was what she'd called it. Van closed his eyes and willed away the memories, but like always, his ghosts from that mission haunted him.

Sweet Cassie, the woman who'd changed everything for him. The first time he saw her with that fucking dick of an uncle, his caveman surfaced, and where Cassie was concerned, he never was able to get that fucker back under control. He was immediately attracted to her shy, sweet smile. The woman never assumed any pretense. She always offered to help, and she worked so damn hard, she made his team look like slackers, and that said one hell of a lot because his team was phenomenal at getting shit done.

His hand drifted down his chest and rubbed the ache between his legs. Because he and Cassie worked the day shift and completed all the routine tasks well before the sun set, he'd started taking her with him on small excursions into the mountains on the pretense of teaching her survival skills. Well, it hadn't started out as a pretense, but after that first kiss...he'd made damn sure there was a reason to get some distance between them and his team. He'd never endanger her or risk exposing his team, so the days when the Hizbul Mujahideen were more active, they stayed hunkered down. But the nights that they could go out a small distance from the camp...those were memories he'd hold forever. Damn, he felt like a lovesick teenager, but just thinking about Cassie made his dick harder than a granite statue dipped in titanium. The memory of the first time she touched him could get him off. He sucked in a lungful of air and grabbed his cock. He remembered it like it had happened five minutes ago.

"What are you going to do when you go back?" Van held her hand as she clambered down the rocky outcropping as they headed to "their" spot—a small cave at the face of the mountain about fifty yards from camp. They could maintain some semblance of privacy and still get back quickly if the need arose. His men never mentioned their frequent trips out in the evening, but he knew they were aware of what was happening between Cassie and

him. They also knew him well enough to know he had serious intentions toward the beautiful puzzle solver.

"I don't know, except that I have to get back to check on my mom." Cassie gave him a sad smile and sat down on a small flat top rock just inside the cave.

Van pulled her to his side and kissed her temple.

"It's a harvest moon tonight." Cassie nodded her chin at the full moon that illuminated the area.

"Harvest moon?"

"Yeah. In Wyoming, where I spent some time, the crops were ready to be harvested, and the hay was ready to be baled about this time every year. The farmers and the ranchers who grew their own feed could see to run the equipment when it was this light. The kids at school called it a harvest moon." She turned to him and bit her bottom lip.

He'd long since learned she did that when she was embarrassed. He watched her in the moonlight as she fought through her shyness to ask him the question on her mind.

"Van?"

"Cassie?" He smiled when she gave a little laugh.

"I want to..." She looked away and bit her lip again.

"You want to what?" God only knew what was on her mind. What he wanted to do wasn't going to happen. They'd already talked, and she'd admitted she

hadn't dated much. That was okay because he was willing to invest the time and any effort. She was well worth any wait...and the blue balls that he'd have to endure. Cassie Valentine was it for him. He knew it in his gut, and he'd learned to trust his instincts, even his baser ones.

"I want to kiss you." She dropped her head to his chest and gave a little squeak as she did.

"Hey, you've kissed me...many times. Why are you acting so shy all of a sudden?"

Cassie shook her head against his collarbone. "No, I want to kiss you...lower."

"Lower?" His dick jumped. She nodded and lifted her hand up his thigh sending every nerve in his body into catastrophic synapsis. He closed his eyes and slammed his jaw together, gritting his teeth for the time it took for his good intentions to crash and burn in an epic flameout. "You don't have to do that." Although his mouth said the words, his mind screamed, 'Yes, please if there is a God in heaven, yes... do that!'

Cassie undid his belt and unbuttoned the front fly of his black battle dress uniform. Even confined by his briefs, his cock sprang forward like a jack-in-the-box that had been wound tight and cranked off. He ran his hands up her arms, trying to anchor himself. Her breath *caught as she lightly ran her finger down the length of his cotton covered shaft. He groaned at the sensation.*

Her head came off his chest, and she looked up into his eyes. "You like that, don't you?"

"Like it? Fuck, no honey. I love it when you touch me."

Cassie smiled that shy smile again and dropped her eyes as she parted the fold of his briefs and pulled him out. "Your skin is so warm and soft, but you're hard. It's really big and thick."

Van laughed, which brought her eyes up to his again.

"Was it wrong to say that?"

"Telling a man he's really big and thick is never the wrong thing to say."

Van cupped his balls and pulled them away from his body. He clamped his eyes shut and flashed to the memory of the first time he'd made love to her. After all those weeks of talking and kissing, the tentative touches grew bolder and more certain...and he'd fallen head-over-fucking heels in love with her. That first night...fuck. He stroked his shaft and let his mind drift.

The moon caressed her white skin with a luminescence that mesmerized him. His fingers traced curves. Her nipple hardened under his thumb and he couldn't resist taking it into his mouth. Her fingers threaded through his hair and kept him there, not that he fought the idea.

"Please, Van, I want you to make love to me. Show me how to make you feel good."

Cassie loosened her grip on his hair and he lifted his head. He could just see her eyes in the moonlight. "Honey, you make me feel good. We don't have condoms and..."

"I won't get pregnant. I had a shot before I met you in Colorado. It is supposed to last for three months."

"Honey, it's more than that. We're in a cave. You deserve better."

"I don't..." She lifted her hand and put a finger to his lips before he could object to her comment. "I want you to make love to me, Van. Show me how to love you. I need this. Us."

Van stroked his cock; the bed springs produced a gentle song under him. Fuck it, he pushed reality away and chased his dream again. Cassie...

Van's lips and fingers memorized the contours of her small body. Her luscious curves and soft skin trembled under his attention. He worshipped her, forgoing his own almost debilitating need for her to ensure her desire was as intense as his. He needed this encounter, their first time together, to be the best she'd ever experience.

She was so different from any relationship he'd ever had. Shy and timid with her touches. She made no demands on him other than her desire for him to make love to her. He lowered over her and took her lips in a kiss. He was tender, seeking and sensual.

Her arms pulled him down on top of her. "Please, Van...I ache. Please."

He took her lips as he lifted her leg and pushed inside her, consuming her surprised cry. Her fingers clawed into his shoulders, stilling him. Brilliant shards of white heat raced down his spine and pooled in his balls. He needed to move, to claim her as his. She was so tight, so hot. He broke their kiss allowing them to consume each other's breath. "Cassie..." He couldn't form any other words.

"Make love to me," she whispered.

Van's body tightened, his back arched as his hand flew up and down his cock. The springs echoed his movement, but he didn't fucking care. He called her name when he came. He didn't care how pathetic it was. *He loved her.* Still. The bitter desolation he lived with crept back in as the evidence of his desire cooled. Why had she left without a word?

CHAPTER 4

"Where the fuck are you?"

Cassie cringed at the anger in her uncle's voice. She'd just finished feeding and changing the baby, and she prayed he would sleep until she had dinner served and the kitchen cleaned. She pulled her threadbare flannel shirt around her shoulders and stepped out into the living room. Her father and uncle turned and glared at her. "Get your ass in the kitchen and put dinner on the table." She nodded and walked to the kitchen quickly, darting away to stay out of reach of her uncle's fists.

She set the table while the men used the sink to clean off the dirt and grime working the mine shaft had left on them. Grabbing the oven mitts off the counter, she pulled their food out of the oven and put it on the table, moving deftly to keep away from her uncle. Her father had never beaten her, but he'd never done a damn thing to keep her from her uncle's rages. She made sure they had everything they needed and retreated to the stool in the corner of the kitchen, sitting down near the old wood-burning oven. It was her corner; where she and her baby spent almost every evening because the residual heat from cooking dinner warmed the kitchen and kept away some of the drafts from the cold mountain nights.

Cassie stared at her fingers, listening to the men eat. She'd be allowed to have anything they didn't eat. She hadn't sat down for a proper meal since her mother had died. How she'd delivered a healthy baby, she'd never know, but her son was beautiful, and for now, healthy.

She glanced at the floorboard that covered the meager stash of items she'd collected. She'd salvaged a small pocket knife her uncle had thrown away. One of the blades was broken, but she'd sharpened the functioning blades to a razor's edge. There were two books of matches wrapped in a small square of wax paper along with a small squirt bottle of kerosene. Two protein bars that had fallen out of the bags her father and uncle had brought to the cabin from the outside were down there, too. The protein bars were a gift from fate. When her uncle and father tallied the inventory of food, they weren't included, so she didn't have to account for them. She had an empty water bottle and two chlorination tabs in that space just waiting for the day she'd have to flee. Those treasures, coupled with whatever she could grab the day she was forced to go, would be all she and her son would have to survive.

She silently thanked God for the time she'd spent on her last assignment with Guardian. The skills she'd learned from Van and his team would help her survive and keep her baby safe. She'd have to leave before the snows started—or before her uncle's rages hurt her too badly.

A low snuffling wail sounded from the small alcove where she'd built Samuel's mat. Cassie jumped forward, but her uncle beat her to the door.

"Oh no. That bastard isn't going to interrupt my dinner. I'll go put that little shit out of my misery. One twist of his neck and I'll have silence."

"No, please, Uncle Carl. Please, let me go to him." Cassie didn't see the backhand that sent her into the cabinets. The explosion of light and agony when her cheek hit the butcher block countertop almost made her pass out, and she would have vomited if she had anything in her stomach. Cassie stifled a cry and tried to crawl toward her son. Her uncle's boot connected with her ribs...again. Cassie couldn't stop her scream of pain. Samuel's wail increased in volume. Cassie scrambled on her hands and knees toward the door. Her uncle kicked her again. His size thirteen boot landed on the back of her thigh. Her leg went numb, but she kept going. She had to get to Samuel before her uncle turned his rage on the innocent baby.

Cassie made it to her child and pulled him into her chest, cowering in the small alcove. She could barely lift him without crying out in pain, but she managed to lift her shirt and put her baby on her breast, comforting him. He immediately fixed on her nipple and quieted. Her silent sobs racked her body. She had to get them out of this hell.

"Lawrence, how many times do I need to say it? That murdering slut and that bastard are worthless. Your wife, God rest her soul, died at *her* hand. That bastard shouldn't be breathing air and neither should that murderous bitch. *They* killed your wife."

Cassie closed her eyes and cried harder. As soon as she returned to the States, she'd used a pregnancy test to confirm her fears. When the results appeared on the slender stick, she'd sunk to the floor in the bathroom of the Atlanta hotel, horror-struck. It had been stupid on her part to ignore the morning sickness and the way her body had changed in the weeks leading up to Sierra team's transition to the States, but she'd been terrified to acknowledge what the symptoms meant. Shame had overwhelmed her at the thought of explaining to Van she was pregnant with his child, that the contraceptive her father and uncle had demanded she receive hadn't worked. Would he think she'd lied to him—that she'd tried to trap him into marriage?

She'd fallen in love with the gentle giant while they'd lived overseas. Van embodied everything she'd ever dreamed of in a man. Love, protection, tenderness and compassion, all the qualities she'd heard existed, but had never witnessed, much less experienced. Her body still ached for his touch, his gentleness. None of it changed what she knew to be true, what she'd heard from his own mouth when the guys bantered back and forth at night. Van did not want a family. Her heart had shattered the second she'd turned her back on him in Atlanta and walked away, but leaving was better than experiencing his condemnation, his almost certain rejection and anger. She'd rather have only good memories of him.

When she had come home pregnant, her religious father had disowned her, and her uncle had taken over the duty of meting out 'discipline'. She remembered curling into a ball to protect her unborn baby from her uncle's relentless punishment. To make matters worse, her mother was punished for Cassie's transgressions, but her mother was beaten by her husband. They were both lucky to survive the months after her return.

Cassie had always lived with abuse. She knew it wasn't right, knew that she and her mother deserved a life without fear and pain. She'd briefly experienced a far different life, but...she closed her eyes. Growing up, her family had lived in Wyoming. She'd gone to high school and learned to play chess with the chess club. Strategy came easily to her. She could picture the moves an opponent would make for the entire game after the first three moves. She never lost. Her club went to regionals, and they won because of her. She went to nationals based on the generosity of her teachers because her father wouldn't pay for the trip. She'd won every match she'd played.

A gentleman from Guardian approached her teacher, who was also her chaperone, and asked if Cassie could look at a word game he'd brought. He said there wasn't a key or a cipher for the game, but he was wondering if she could unscramble it. The teacher called back to Wyoming to ask her parents, and her mother gave permission. Cassie solved the puzzle within eight hours. Guardian sent her mom and dad a check for ten thousand dollars. That was the start of her work for Guardian.

Three times since then, she'd answered a request from Guardian. Each time it was harder to come back to her family—to live without utilities, running water, or indoor plumbing—to live in constant fear. Her father and uncle had bought a small patch of land in the Bitterroot Mountains of Montana and had found a trace of gold. The two men used every dime Cassie earned to sink a shaft deep into the earth, chasing the elusive vein of gold that would make them rich. Her father had threatened to beat her mother to death if Cassie didn't return to the mountaintop or if she told anyone "lies" about exactly what happened in that remote Montana cabin.

The physical threats against her mother had made her return to this wretched cabin in the Bitterroot Mountains. She'd known what was waiting for her on top of the mountain, but she'd needed to do what she could to protect her mom. After Kashmir, she'd tried to leave. She'd begged her mother to come down the mountain with her. She'd explained she could have a full-time job if she wanted it, and that she'd found a man who treated her with respect. She told her mom all about Van. What she couldn't tell her mom was why she'd left him to come back. Her mother didn't need that guilt.

Her mother was only forty-five, but the life her father had forced on them all had taken its toll on the small, fragile woman. Cassie numbed at the memory of her mother begging her to stay on the mountain with her. Her mother swore she'd be able to make Cassie's father understand. Three weeks later, after her mother suffered yet another beating for trying to protect Cassie and her unborn child, her mom finally begged her to leave, to find a safe place. Cassie ultimately agreed out of fear for the life that grew inside her. The next day, as soon as the men left for the shaft, Cassie headed down the mountain.

Her mother must have had a change of heart, because she'd packed a small bag and attempted to follow. Cassie'd managed the climb down the bald face of granite that led to the flatter land below when she'd heard her mom's scream. She scrambled back to find her mom lying at the base of the granite face, broken and dying. She had no idea why her mom had attempted the sheer drop off when the trail cut into the mountain to the right led down a far less challenging descent.

Cassie blinked back, her mother's dying plea echoed through her mind. "Leave me, please, baby. Run, go and don't look back."

"It's okay, momma. I'll get you down the mountain. I'll get you help." Cassie held her mom, the woman's small broken body convulsed.

"Go, hurry. I'm so sorry...I tried." She took her last breath in Cassie's arms.

In her grief, she didn't hear her uncle's approach. The man beat her and then strangled her until she blacked out. Cassie came to as he dragged her back to the cabin, beat her again, and locked her in the small wood closet on the back porch—all the while screaming at her that she was the reason her mother was dead. Sometimes, she thought he was right. If she'd tried harder, if she'd stayed, maybe her mom would be alive.

She'd only thought she'd lived in hell before. Life in true hell began that day. Since then, she'd been starved and the beatings from her uncle increased in severity. Still, she'd managed to survive and, with no help from either of the men, deliver her baby. Her strength had waned to the point her uncle and father no longer feared she'd run. Besides, as her uncle had taunted when he'd taken all her shoes, who would take an infant down the mountain barefoot...unarmed, alone? No one. Both her father and her uncle knew it. Coyotes, wolves, bears, lynx and mountain lions hunted in the dense forests. She heard their cries at night. The dangers for a woman without a gun, carrying an infant, were too many to count. But she'd accept the risk of probable death from exposure or those predators over her certainty she and Samuel would die if they stayed. Protecting her son from her family had become her only focus.

Cassie flinched as chairs scraped the floor in the kitchen. She pulled Samuel closer and turned in toward the wall to protect them both as the men walked past.

"Clean the kitchen, slut, and keep that bastard quiet or *I* will kill it." An unprecedented level of fear shook her to her core. The rough, threatening voice was her *father*—not her uncle. Cassie braced herself on the wall and stood while still holding Samuel. Despite her weakness and the continual tremors, she couldn't calm down, she must escape —now. Her father had never threatened her or Samuel before. He'd never protected them, but his threat tonight ignited a powder keg. If her father gave her uncle any indication he'd allow the man to carry out his threats unopposed, neither she nor Samuel would live to see the next sunset.

Cassie tied an old shirt into a sling and snugged Samuel close to her, so she could keep him warm and quiet. Gingerly, she washed her swollen face, blotting the blood off her cheek. Tomorrow, she'd take Samuel and escape down the mountain.

In the meantime, she needed to keep her uncle and father pacified. Before she cleaned the kitchen, she used a small piece of bread to wipe up all the meat juices from her father's plate. She ate the fat from the meat that he'd cut off and licked off the gravy left on her uncle's plate. She ate the food baked in the small Dutch oven the same way and filled her mouth with the meager amounts of food left in the serving bowls. Cassie walked on the floorboard that concealed the supplies for her escape. It had never been *if* she would leave, but *when*. The when had come.

The front door slammed as either her father or uncle went out to use the outhouse before they went to sleep. The low light of the oil lamp cast a flickering glow against the back wall of the kitchen. The cold breeze did little to still her fears about taking Samuel down the mountain, but she had no choice. She'd run out of time.

Cassie made her way to the corner and slowly slid down the wall onto her little stool. She rubbed Samuel's back and hummed quietly. The front door slammed open again and she jumped, startling the baby. She quietly hushed him and rocked him, although her ribs screamed for her to stop. Heavy boots moved from the front of the cabin to the rear. A door slammed, and the noises in the cabin subsided again.

If she could get to civilization, she could contact the people she knew at Guardian. She could call Jewell King. The woman had been her friend...sort of? She was just as socially awkward as Cassie, kindred spirits her mother would have said. She'd met Jewell King while on her second job for Guardian. They'd become awkward friends, but friends nonetheless.

God, she wished she could call Jewell. The last time they'd spoken was just before she'd come back up into the mountains. Cassie had called her from the pay phone at the diner in Buckskin Junction. Their conversation that day was etched in her mind.

"Why won't you tell Van you're pregnant?" Jewell demanded for the fifth or sixth time.

"Because I can't. I screwed up. I didn't think I could get pregnant, and to be honest, I listened when he and his men talked. Believe me, he doesn't want a family. Besides, Van never told me he loved me, nor did he mentioned a future after we got back to the States. Maybe after my baby is born, I'll seek him out."

"You said your folks are really religious and strict. Maybe you should come stay with me and figure something out."

"I can't. I have two days to make it up the mountain before they..." Cassie'd seen too much to doubt her father would beat her mother into the ground. She cleared her throat and continued, "I think I'll ask my mom to come down the mountain and live with me. I know my dad and uncle won't approve, but my mom... Jewell, I can't leave her up there alone. As much as I

love doing these jobs for you, I hate being away from her when I go on assignment for Guardian. She's frail, and the work is so hard."

"Are you going to be alright?" Jewell's concern seeped through the telephone connection, tangible and not unwelcome.

Cassie was silent as she debated how honestly to answer her question. "Yeah, I should be. I'll leave if I feel unsafe."

"Okay, but I'm holding you to a promise to get word to me about you and the baby. Snail mail, email, telephone...hell, carrier pigeon or dog sled. Us geeks have to stick together. The puzzle master is important to me. You are important to a lot of people here at Guardian."

When Guardian wanted her to solve another puzzle, they would contact her on the old ham radio her father used to have in the small living area of the cabin. When she'd finally been allowed unrestricted access to the cabin after her mom died, the radio was gone. No doubt so she couldn't call for help. She hadn't been able to send word, and if she could have, what would she have said? What could Jewell do? Dispatch Guardian to storm the mountain? She wasn't valuable enough to be a priority...to anyone. She was a freelance puzzle solver and nothing more. As her father and uncle told her repeatedly, there were hundreds of people just like her. She wasn't special. She didn't matter to a huge organization like Guardian...nevertheless, she shivered, curled around her baby, and sent up a silent prayer. *"Dear God, please...if we ever get off this mountain, please let Jewell answer her phone."*

Cassie shuddered and shook her head, clearing it of useless wishes. She rubbed Samuel's little rump, up his back and back down. The methodic touch relaxed not only him, but her, too. She allowed herself the comfort of thinking about Van, of wondering where he might be. If he was safe. Samuel's daddy was devastatingly handsome, and he had been kind to her. The man was six-feet-three-inches tall with the silkiest dark brown hair, the most compassionate hazel eyes, and a soft, full beard. With his tattoos and bulk, he could pass as a rogue biker, but Cassie knew the intelligence and warmth beneath the scary veneer. She prayed that Samuel would grow up to be like his father. Her uncle's snores drifted through the small cabin into the kitchen where she sat. She prayed he'd get the chance to grow up.

CHAPTER 5

"Okay, these guys will get you where you're going. Jasper here rides double if the woman decides to come down the mountain with you. The pack horse is a stubborn beast, but he'll keep up with you. You've got the GPS coordinates?" Isiah Reichs swung the horse trailer door closed and Sampson Waters brought down the catch bar, sealing it shut.

"We do." Van held up a five-inch by eight-inch tablet with the GPS coordinates entered. It was overlaid with the latest satellite imagery and also functioned as a satellite phone. Both Travis and Van had one that slid into the protected front shoulder pocket of their ultra-thin bullet-proof vests. Van opened the back end of the

Guardian SUV and unlocked their traveling arsenal.

A low whistle sounded right before Reichs and Waters stepped up to inspect the weapons within.

"Did you come here to fight a war?" Waters grabbed a rifle out of the rack. "Fuck me standing...an ESR?"

"Damn straight, that's an XM2010 Enhanced Sniper Rifle." Travis grabbed his two .45s and loaded them, chambering a round in each pistol.

"What the fuck does this thing fire?" Reichs grabbed the rifle from Waters and brought it up taking aim down the valley.

".300 Winchester Magnum." Van picked up the ammo for the weapon and an empty magazine. He loaded the rounds as the two men took turns admiring the weapon.

"What's the range on this?" Sampson laid the weapon back in its resting spot.

Van glanced up at him and smiled. "I think you know."

"Yeah, I do. 1200 meters, but not effective after a thousand."

"It's effective." Travis pulled out an Interceptor 911 and slid it into the scabbard attached to the back of his vest.

"I've never heard of a shot farther than a thousand with this weapon." Waters crossed his arms and watched as they armed up.

"Trust me, it's effective." Van looked up at the man and gave him a dead-on stare. At thirteen hundred meters, he'd taken out a murdering son of a bitch who'd just killed three women and two children. It was effective.

"Just how dangerous is this woman?" Reichs asked as he watched Van and Travis pull their weapons out of the arsenal.

"It isn't the woman we are worried about. It's the bears." Van said with a serious expression. Holding the smile off his face was a tough job. Van and Travis put in their earpieces. They'd activate them if they were separated. The comms mic was built into the vest collar.

"Right." Waters and Reichs busted up laughing. "Seriously, what is with the armament?"

"Standard issue. We are going into an area in which we don't have proper intel. As a recognized, national law enforcement entity, we are cleared to carry all this. I'd rather have it than need it."

Isiah Reichs tipped his cowboy hat back and looked up at the sky. "Well, damn it the next time Guardian pulls me back into civilization, I'll have to ask for some better toys." His eyes fell to Van and he got deadly serious. "You might make it up the lower third of the mountain by nightfall and if you ride hard, maybe halfway. Build yourself a good enough fire, and the animals won't be an issue, but the people back there in those hills? They are hardcore. I wish you luck."

Van threw the keys to the Guardian SUV to Waters. "I'll call you when we need a ride back. Take care of her for me?" He nodded toward the SUV.

"Damn straight. I can't wait to play around with all the shit in this vehicle." Sampson headed toward the driver's side door.

Van picked up his rifle. He closed the gun safe and then the rear door of the vehicle. "Hey, Sampson?"

"Yo!" The man leaned out the driver's side door.

"You can play with, fire, test or have fun with anything in the truck, just don't touch the red button under the panel on the dash." Van looped the reins over his horse's neck and stepped up into the saddle.

"Why? Will rockets launch out of the rear end of this thing?" They all laughed at the comment.

"Nah, man. That duress button will activate an

alarm bringing in every law enforcement agency, and any Guardian, posted in the tri-state area."

"Are there that many Guardians way out here in the Midwest?" Isiah Reichs leaned on the back of his truck, giving Van some serious consideration.

"Nowadays? A lot more than you'd think." Van winked and turned his horse, nudging the animal into a trot. Travis's horse fell into step, and they headed west into the Bitterroot Mountains.

CHAPTER 6

*C*assie carried Samuel in the sling she'd knotted around her neck. She'd nursed him before her father and uncle had stirred and made their way into the kitchen for their breakfasts. She'd made the men's lunch and placed the food in a bucket covered with a small piece of fabric to keep the dirt and bugs out. She'd cut up several rashers of side pork, fried it and added two eggs each from the laying chickens she tended. The eggs were her primary protein. As long as she had four eggs every morning, the men didn't track the fact she ate any extra she'd gathered. She fried two large slices of bread in the bacon grease and put the food on the table minutes before the men walked into the room. Cassie walked over to the corner and sat on the stool. Her heart hammered in her chest. Today was the day. She and Samuel were leaving, and it scared her, but not as much as staying. She rubbed Samuel's back, keeping him quiet.

She couldn't defend herself, or Samuel, from her uncle. Most of the time he just stared at her. The hatred her father's brother harbored for her battled another emotion she saw in his eyes. One that Cassie never wanted to acknowledge. Her uncle would kill her someday, but she feared what he would do to her before he took her life. However, none of that would matter after today. She would gather her precious items and head down the mountain and find a way to live free from fear.

Cassie gave a visible jump when the men rose from the table. She kept her eyes lowered and watched their feet, making sure to keep Samuel out of her uncle's way. They left without a word. Nothing new there, but when she glanced up, the look her uncle and father threw at her before they left let her know her time had run out. Cassie drew a steadying breath and went about cleaning the kitchen as she would every morning in case they came back to check on her. It rarely happened, but sometimes her uncle returned. Those times terri-fied Cassie. The sun crested the ridge over the top of the mountain. Following the plan, she'd mentally rehearsed a thousand times, she opened the front door and stepped out into the sunshine still carrying Samuel. There was no birdsong. Someone or something was out there, close enough and big enough to stop the animal noises. She picked up the feed bucket and went about tending the chickens. Her eyes scanned the dense foliage the men had pushed back away from the house. Cassie finished her chore and went back inside. She grabbed the broom and went into the kitchen just as the front door slammed open. Her father walked into the kitchen and stood in the doorway staring at her.

Cassie backed up, moving to keep Samuel away from his eyes. "What do you need me to do?" She didn't make the mistake of calling him father. She wasn't his daughter anymore. He was convinced she was the spawn of hell and the reason his wife was dead.

"Die." The man spun on his heel and exited the cabin. Cassie leaned out carefully to watch him walk away. Her entire body trembled with a fear so consuming she felt faint. She bent down and lifted the floorboard in the kitchen and pulled out her supplies. She grabbed a half loaf of bread and sliced off a huge chunk, slathered it in butter and ate it as she built a pack. She wouldn't be here for the beating eating their food would bring. If they caught her, the food would be the least of her worries. Cassie ate and drank until she couldn't consume anymore. God only knew how long she'd need to make the supplies she had last. She took Samuel out of the sling and changed him before she added the remainder of the homemade cloth diapers into the sling, adding warmth and padding to the thin material. She grabbed her essentials, filled the bottle with good well water and dropped everything except the knife into another sling that she draped across her chest and then dropped down her back. She went to the door and cracked it. A robin's song caressed her ears. Cassie shut the door behind her and made her way around the area the chickens roosted as if she were hunting for eggs before she slid into the foliage and headed east. She kept her steps steady and fast, but not fast enough to cause destruction along the trail. If her uncle or father came after her, she wasn't going to give them any indication of where she'd gone.

Van pulled the reins on his horse and stopped where the trail widened into a high valley. They'd made it up the mountain about halfway, but the sun was setting, and as soon as it dipped below the ridge in the west, it would be too dangerous to keep riding. He didn't need to say anything to Travis. The man made his way to the flat area beside a stand of trees and got down to business. They had a fire started, and their gear readied for the night before darkness fell. After so many missions, splitting the workload came naturally. Van pulled off the tack from the animals and took them all to a small stream that cut through the middle of the meadow. He let the horses drink their fill before highlining them out for the night. They had room to forage for grass and still be close enough that Van and Travis could protect them from anything that thought horseflesh would make a good meal.

When he made it back to camp, Travis had two MREs open and steaming. Tablets dropped into pouches made the water they added boil and heat the meal inside.

"What did I draw?" Van sat down and stretched out his legs in front of him."

Travis threw him the outside bag. "Beef stew for both of us, so I don't want to hear any complaints."

"Did you already eat my peanut butter?" Travis had probably consumed the crackers, too. The man was a bottomless pit.

"You don't like peanut butter."

"How the hell would I know? I never get to eat it."

"You told me once."

Travis handed him his pouch, and they fished out the packets of food. Eating MREs would add about twelve hundred calories to your day, but the meals were murder on the digestive system. They reclined against their saddles and fed the fire with the remnants of a small dead tree they'd found not too far from where they camped.

"Dude, it never ceases to amaze me the number of stars you can see away from the lights of a city. Reminds me of Kashmir."

Van slid a look over at his best friend and purposefully ignored the Kashmir comment. He waved at the mountains as he spoke, "This whole country can make you feel small. I remember once when I was visiting my grand…" Van froze. Travis lifted away from his saddle, and the horse's heads popped up, their ears twitching from the front to the side. "Did you hear that?"

Travis held up a hand and whispered, "I don't know what the fuck it was, but I heard it." They sat motionless for what seemed like an eternity before they heard it again. "Dude, that's a baby's cry."

"No fucking way. Maybe a big cat? I've heard they can sound like a baby crying." Van couldn't imagine a baby out here in the wilderness. They waited, and once again the plaintive cry of an infant traveled across the meadow. "Fuck me. That *is* a kid."

"Skipper?" Travis's question echoed his own. What the fuck were they going to do? If that child's cry this far out in the wilderness wasn't a literal cry for help, he didn't know what was.

Van pulled out his GPS and called up the satellite overview of where they were currently resting. Travis leaned over so he could see. "We're here. There is a ridgeline there, I'd think maybe there would be a possibility of caves up there. If we have a family holed up in a bunch of caves, I'm sure the rangers and wardens in the area would want to know about it. Besides, Reichs gave us enough supplies to last over a week. We have two more days up here, max."

"I'll load the extra supplies on your horse." Travis was making the same call as he was. After years of working together, they thought alike.

Van nodded. "You take the pack horse with you up to Valentines' property and deliver the message. I'll meet you here, tomorrow night at sundown."

"We are staying in contact with the comms, Skipper. I got a bad feeling about this shit." Travis drank the rest of his water out of his canteen cup and hunkered down on his saddle.

"Not sure how good the reception will be with the mountain between us." Van glanced up at the glaring granite face of the mountain.

"Then pop off a round and I'll hightail it back down here." Travis rolled over, finished with the conversation. "Night, Skipper."

Van stood first watch, adding firewood as the flames consumed the logs. He'd give Travis four solid hours before he woke him to take over. They'd be awake and ready to go when the sun crested.

He listened intently for another cry but was unable to hear anything except the normal song of the night. He hoped the family would welcome the welfare check and the addition of some supplies to whatever stores they had. He stood up and stretched, moving out to check on the horses. He spoke to them, low and soothing, so they knew he was approaching. He could see the camp and still carried all his weaponry as he searched the darkness for unseen threats. It was ingrained training that was as instinctual as breathing.

He rubbed the nose of the mount he'd been riding today. "Where the hell is that baby?" He whispered his question to the horse. It nuzzled into his hand. "The reports said the only people living up here were the Valentines, but someone else has to be up here. The cabin is another half-day's ride from here. There's no way that sound carried from where they are." Van chuckled when the horse pushed him away with his head. "Alright, I'll leave you alone. You're obviously not a night owl." He wandered over to a large outcropping of granite and stared into the darkness. His thoughts drifted to Cassie, as they usually did. The anger he used to feel had died, albeit slowly. The hurt...well, that hadn't lessened. It lodged in the middle of his chest, and he lived with it every day.

He circled the camp and made his way back to

where Travis slept. A simple hand on his shoulder brought Travis out of his sleep and instantly alert.

"All's quiet." Van laid his rifle down as Travis picked his up.

"No more crying?"

"Nothing."

"Roger that. I'll wake you in four." Travis threw another log on the fire and drifted off into the darkness. Van listened to his quiet footfall recede. He closed his eyes and, with the practiced skill of countless missions, he slept.

Cassie wrapped her father's lined flannel shirt that she'd used to build her backpack around both her and Samuel. Her back was against the wall of a small cave...more likely a slight indention in the face of the granite wall, but it had a small overhang, and she could see all the ways her uncle or father could approach. Before the sunset, she had a partial view of the valley below her. There were deer in the middle, grazing lazily until something startled them. They fled toward her, so the threat, probably an animal, was between her and freedom. She searched the area she could see for movement, but she saw nothing.

The moon's light painted the landscape with a glow that illuminated the granite. It reminded her of the long nights in Kashmir. She remembered every time Van had led her out away from the camp. The tender touches, soft kisses and warmth of his body holding her were as vivid tonight as they were over a year ago. She gently rocked her baby. He squirmed and chewed on his fist as her memories led her away from the Montana mountain top, back to a cave in a distant country.

Van had captured her heart. She had no defenses against the kindness and tenderness he'd lavished on her. Cassie smiled into the night as she remembered when she decided Van would be her first. Moisture grew in her eyes as she recalled making the decision. She wanted to have that experience with Van. She'd seen the way her uncle's eyes traveled after her and stripped her of any decency. In her gut she knew what he wanted. The thought of being violated by her own uncle was sickening and repulsive...and inevitable. But she'd had to come back to this mountain. There'd been no other option for her. There had never been. Her uncle or her father would have killed her mom if she hadn't returned.

She'd asked Van to make love to her because she trusted him to make it beautiful. Cassie wiped at the tears that fell and glanced up at the moon. That special night was hers and hers alone. For once in her life she'd been selfish. No amount of abuse could strip away the memories of his touch, the look in his eyes, or the safety she'd felt in the shelter of his body. She glanced down at her son. Unfortunately, Samuel was destined to pay the price. She glanced out over the meadow. Her escape must succeed.

Exhaustion haunted her, and Samuel was fussy, which was rare for the babe. He was used to being carried in the sling. She patted his back, talking to him in hushed whispers. The chill of the night air would carry her voice and any noises anyone following her would make. Cassie drank all the water in her bottle, knowing she could fill it tomorrow morning and use the tablet to chlorinate it and make the water safe for the last leg of her journey. There was a stream at the other end of the meadow. When Samuel let out a cry, Cassie hurriedly stripped out of her slings and tried to bare her breast. She bounced him gently, but her fingers fumbled in her rush. He cried out again, rooting at her chest, looking for her nipple. She shushed him and pulled at her shirt, lifting it, but Samuel wasn't going to be pacified. His cry echoed loudly against the rock face she'd backed against. Cassie managed to free herself and snuggle her baby on her breast. She carefully held him with one arm while she grabbed her precious supplies with the other.

She had to move. If her uncle or father was following her, then Samuel had given them a compass to find her. Dark fell quickly. Cassie stopped at the end of the ghost trail she'd been following and searched for a place to hide for the night. The area didn't provide many options. The tree line was thin, and there were too many open spaces—spaces that could be viewed from above. She worked her way into a gnarled mass of branches between a small stand of trees and prayed the branches would obscure them. She nursed and soothed Samuel until he fell asleep. Cassie placed him on her chest and burped him before she leaned back. The injuries to her face, ribs, and thigh ached, but the keeping little Samuel's body warm was the only thing that mattered. She draped the sling holding the spare diapers over him and settled back.

She gazed up at the multitude of stars and wondered what life would have been like if she'd stayed with Van. She shook her head. Staying hadn't been an option. Instead, Cassie had sentenced her mom to death when she fled down the mountain. Guilt and remorse ate at her. She wasn't a murderer like her uncle claimed, but her mother's death was a result of her actions, even though she hadn't known her mother had followed. What had changed her mother's mind? The tearful goodbye? The fervent plea for her mom to leave with her? Cassie shook her head as the questions she'd never have answered ricocheted through her mind. She'd been resolute about staying when Cassie'd left that morning.

Cassie heard a long scratching rattle of rocks to her left. Something large was coming down the mountain. The sound was distant, but in her gut, she knew it wasn't an animal. She closed her eyes, hugged her son to her and prayed for a miracle.

CHAPTER 7

"You're sure you don't want to go up to the cabin, Skipper?" Travis mounted his horse and looked down at him as Van tightened the cinch on his saddle. "You could maybe get some answers."

"I got all the answers I needed when she left me high and dry." He grabbed the reins on his mount's neck and lifted into the saddle. "You take the message to her. If she comes back with you, fine. If she doesn't, then we did our job. I'm going to find that baby and make sure whoever is out here is alright."

"Roger that." Travis turned his horse and headed up the mountain. Before Van nudged his horse forward into the meadow, his friend called back over his shoulder. "Tonight. At sunset. Right here. If you aren't waiting, I'll call it in."

"The same goes for you. Why are we having this conversation? Stop talking and start riding." Van laughed at the middle finger Travis threw over his shoulder. Travis was a mother hen and that was what made him one hell of an XO. One day the guy would have his own team. It would suck for Van, but Travis deserved a team of his own. He needed to make that recommendation when he got back to civilization.

Van pulled up at the tree line and took in the massive granite face at the back end of the meadow. He could see a small trail, a feathering of lighter white on the face of the rock. If there were caves up there, he couldn't see them, but that cry had to have come from somewhere. He pulled out his GPS again and reoriented himself with the topography. If he headed straight down the middle of the pasture, he might scare off the people he was looking to help. It figured if they were up here and hiding, seeing a person coming straight at them would send them hightailing it into areas he couldn't follow. He turned his mount back into the trees and headed toward the creek. He'd follow the water through the trees as far as he could and then move to the west, keeping out of sight from above. The closer he could get to the family before they discovered him, the more likely he would be able to make contact.

Van tracked the stream for over an hour. The meandering cut of the water took him through some of the most gorgeous country he'd ever seen. He was downwind of the deer grazing in the meadow and was far enough away that they weren't spooked as he slowly guided his horse through the trees. Granite outcroppings forced him to alter his route away from the water's edge on numerous occasions, but the roundabout way kept him out of sight.

He would have made the bottom of the mountain if he'd ridden straight up the valley, but every instinct told him he needed to keep hidden. His gut told him that an infant this far up meant trouble. He didn't know what he'd run into, but he would be ready. His sidearm rested comfortably in its holster, and his rifle wasn't secured in its boot. He rode with the balls of his feet on the stirrups ready to kick out and dive off the horse should the parents of the baby have a sudden, violent objection to his arrival.

He skirted a clearing about three-quarters of

the way down the huge meadow and stopped. A person was making his way down the face of the rock in front of him. Van lifted the rifle and looked through the scope. There was a determination in his stride as the man descended. He wasn't pussy-footing around. He was making time, and he was coming fast. Instinctively he knew this man was dangerous. What if there wasn't a family up here, but a woman who was escaping with a baby…from the man coming down the face of the cliff now. Fuck. There were too many variables. One thing Van did know for a fact, he wouldn't be able to help anyone if he didn't get closer. He nudged his horse into a trot and picked out the quickest way to the face of the rock without revealing himself.

Cassie woke with a start. She'd fallen asleep. Samuel lay on her chest; his long dark lashes lay delicately against his cheeks as he nursed on his fist as he slept. She could feel dampness from his diaper. Cassie carefully examined the area. The sun shone over the ridge to the east of the valley almost halfway up to the zenith. She must have slept for hours after nursing Samuel in the predawn morning. The last thing she remembered was thinking about Van, wishing for things that could never be.

Cassie carefully sat up and laid Samuel down on a soft bed of leaves. She changed his diaper, tucking the soiled one into a rotted-out tree trunk. If her uncle and father were following her, she needed to be careful. She smiled and talked to Samuel as he woke. Her voice a mere whisper, but her baby responded kicking his legs and waving his arms in the air. Even in his desperate circumstances, Samuel was a happy baby. Cassie took a bite of one of the protein bars and cringed at the chalky taste. The water bottle was empty, but she could rectify that in short order. The creek should be within a half-hour's walk. She let Samuel nurse as she finished her bar, nearly choking on the last bite because her mouth was so dry.

She gathered her possessions, put Samuel into his sling and worked her way out of the leaves that obscured her from view. Unfortunately, the branches obscured her vision as well. Cassie stood up and stretched as far as she could once she moved past the small thicket of trees. She looked up at the ridge and froze. Her uncle was coming down the trail. She bolted back into the trees, but she knew...he'd seen her. She moved quickly through the trees not even trying to hide the route she took. Her only chance now was to get to civilization. Her uncle was a brute of a man. Her one advantage was his bulk made him slow.

Cassie headed into the trees. The branches pulled at her thin clothes, tearing the fabric as she race-walked through the thickets. Her hands and arms covered Samuel protecting him from the environment. Cassie's heart pounded. There was no way she could make it out of the valley. She needed a place to hide until her uncle tired of searching for her or believed her to be gone, but she didn't have enough food to do that. She glanced back and missed ducking away from a branch. It cut through her sleeve, and she gasped as she tightened her grip on Samuel. He startled at her movement and started to wail. She heard her uncle's raging yell behind her. Oh God, he was so much closer than she thought. Cassie searched for a place to hide as she ran with Samuel clutched to her chest. She broke out of the trees and stumbled. Tucking and turning so she fell on her back she screamed when her shoulder hit an outcropping of granite. Samuel's cries and hers echoed in down the valley. Cassie tried to get up and hold her baby, but pain shot in hot pokers down her arm. She checked Samuel over quickly making sure he was okay. His face was red, and he screamed at the top of his lungs. His arms and legs kicked and flew about. Thank God, it seemed other than being mad or scared, he was alright. Holding him with her good arm, Cassie braced against a tree and tried to stand as she searched for a place to hide him from her uncle. She had to get him to safety.

CHAPTER 8

*V*an dug his heels into his horse, and they launched from the tree line. His mount raced like a bat out of hell heading toward the face of the rock. He heard a woman's scream at the same time the child's cries made it to his ears. The big bastard that clambered down the mountain had entered the trees to the west, and that was where Van raced. He let the horse have its head and lowered over the saddle. He grabbed one of his forty-fives out of its holster and squeezed the grip, neutralizing the safety on the weapon. The only sounds he heard were the pounding of his horse's hooves as they raced the twelve hundred yards that separated him from the base of the mountain.

Van caught sight of the man and flicked the

reins of his horse's bridle sending them into the trees again. It was the most direct route to his destination. The horse jumped a fallen, decaying tree and raced through the smaller trees as if the hounds of hell were at its heels. Van crouched, keeping his center low, so the horse didn't have to work as hard. He saw the man approaching a smaller person who was propped against a tree. The small figure lifted a hand as if that would keep the menacing figure at bay. The bastard lifted an arm and swung, sending the smaller figure to the forest floor.

The screams of the infant grew louder as he approached. Van lifted his weapon and aimed. The bastard must have heard his horse's approach because he looked up. Van hesitated for a moment as he realized he *knew* that son of a bitch. He leveled the gun and squeezed the trigger, purpose-fully missing the man and the person he'd jerked off the ground. The shot echoed throughout the valley. Travis would hear it, and he'd be hightailing it back to his location, but Van didn't have the luxury of immediate backup. The horse Reichs had given him was true and steady even when the weapon fired. He kicked his feet out of the stirrups and hung low over the side of the saddle making himself a difficult target if the fucker had a gun. Van timed his jump. His horse tore through the small clearing where the man held the smaller person. His fist lifted again, and Van shot. The smaller person dropped like a rock, and the man who held them stood unmoving above the pile at his feet. Van knew his aim was true, but with the movement of the horse, he prayed he'd hit his target and not the victim.

As the horse approached Van leveled his gun again and pulled the reins, sending his mount into a sliding stop. Van vaulted out of the saddle and charged the fucker, landing with his shoulder against the bastard's gut.

The big man raged and swung out with hands the size of small boulders. Van continued to roll past the bastard, forcing the man to miss. He sprung to his feet ready to put the fucker down. He noticed blood soaking the man's shirt. Van didn't know if it belonged to him or the person he'd been holding, and he didn't have time to play doctor. The larger man lifted to his feet quicker than Van would imagine he was capable of moving and then dropped into a fighting stance. Van didn't wait for the asshole to strike first. He moved in and landed a combination left hook and a right uppercut to the jaw before he dropped and swept the big fucker's legs out from underneath him. The son of a bitch went down, and when he hit the ground, he stayed down. Van moved quickly, instinct and training taking over. The brute was a brawler, but Van had been trained by the Marines and then by Guardian. The asshole didn't have a chance. Van dropped a knee on the man's back and grabbed his arm, wrenching it behind his back. He pulled a zip-tie cable from his vest and secured his wrists before he lifted off the dazed man. Gripping his jacket, Van rolled the asshole over and made sure he wouldn't bleed out, but only because it was ingrained through years of training. Van didn't give a flying fuck if the man expired. He saw the through and through wound his bullet caused. No arterial bleeding. The fucker would live until he made sure...

Van swung and scurried on his knees to the smaller person. He saw the mass of blonde hair and he...knew. Carefully, he turned the woman over and pushed her hair out of her face. Bruises marred her beauty, and they weren't all new. The split lip, the swelling knot on her jaw and the lump on the side of her head were from this altercation...maybe. The rest? Damn it, what the fuck was going on?

He examined Cassie's bruised and swollen face. He could see her pulse beating strong in the column of her neck, but that bastard hit her hard enough to knock her out. Fuck, she was so skinny. A gusty wail from an infant drew Van's attention from Cassie to the far side of the small clearing. He carefully moved away from Cassie after glancing at the bastard he'd cuffed to make sure he was still secure. Van kept one eye on the man who was now stirring as he scrambled to where he heard the child crying. He had to reach under a fallen tree, but he was able to gently remove the baby. It was wrapped tightly in damp, ragged fabric, not a blanket. He had no idea how to hold the kid, but he knew enough to support the baby's back and head. Thank you, television. Van tucked the child to his chest, careful to hold the kid's head and moved back toward Cassie.

The baby settled and stopped crying almost immediately. Van glared at the fucker across the small dirt clearing. That *was* her uncle. The man who'd dropped her off in Denver before their mission. He remembered. He hated the son of a bitch then, and now...well, he was fighting the urge to kill the fucker.

Van fell back against a log, near where Cassie lay. The child was young. He had no idea how to gauge how young, but it wasn't old enough to be on its own, that was for damn sure, and Van was useless with kids. He pulled out his sat phone and activated his comms.

"What the fuck happened?" He winced as Travis's voice bellowed over the comms.

"It's Cassie. She was trying to get away from her uncle. The bastard attacked her before I got to her."

"Is she alright?"

He could tell by the way the wind thrummed through the comms that Travis's horse was traveling fast.

"He knocked her out. Her pulse is strong. I've got the kid."

"Wait, Cassie has a kid?"

"Tiny one."

"Fuck me."

"Yeah."

"Did you make it to the homestead?"

"Nope, I was about a half mile away. I could see

it, but when I heard the weapon's report, I headed back. I'm about an hour away."

"Don't kill the horse. Reichs will skin you alive. I've got the situation contained. I'm calling Guardian to get a helicopter in here to pick us up." Van surveyed the meadow. Damn he hoped they had, or could get, a pilot brave enough or stupid enough to land a copter up here. There was no way Cassie needed to ride down this mountain.

"I'll slow the horses down and give them a breather. I'll get ahold of Reichs and have him contact the local authorities."

"Copy that. We are at the base of that massive granite wall at the south end of the meadow."

"I'll be there ASAP. Keep your comms on, Skipper."

"Roger that. Hey...what do you know about kids?" Van looked down at the baby who was squirming in his arms.

"According to my sister, who has a small army, you keep them fed, keep them dry, and keep them warm." Travis laughed. "So, change it, and wrap it up in something warm, but unless you have a milk cow around or Cassie has some bottles with her, keeping the kid fed might be a problem."

Van nodded even though Travis couldn't see

him. He checked on Cassie again before he pulled up his satellite phone and called in the Calvary. The conversation lasted twenty seconds tops, but he had help inbound and they would be there at first light in the morning.

Van put the phone away and looked down at the bundle in his arms. Why would Cassie be down here with her baby? Van's hand shook as he lifted the blanket off the little one's face. The child blinked up at him and wiggled his arm out of his cloth cocoon. It took a moment to sink in, but what he was looking at? Cassie had a child. She'd left him and what...immediately hooked up with someone else? That made no sense. No matter what, he *knew* Cassie wouldn't, no, couldn't have been that callous. She had to have cared for him. God knew he loved her. He glanced over at her. He still loved her.

The baby was tiny. It couldn't be that old. Van did a quick calculation and he balked at his conclusion. He tapped the tip of each finger counting back the months. *Holy shit.* Could this be *his* child?

Van's phone vibrated. He answered the call feeling like he'd fallen down a rabbit hole.

CHAPTER 9

assie couldn't outrun the monsters chasing her. Samuel was crying. She could hear him, but she couldn't find him. What had they done? She screamed his name, but she had no voice. She had to find him. She had to save him! *"It's alright. I've got your baby. He's fine."* Van...no, God this was a dream...somehow, she knew that. Van's voice? Why was he here? Cassie pushed against the darkness. She had to get to him. She had to find Samuel, to get him away from those monsters.

Consciousness slammed into her with the impact of a baseball bat swung at full force. Her mind exploded with terror, coating everything in a film of horror.

Samuel! She had to find her baby! Panic took her breath away. She pushed up and rolled onto her hands and knees a mere second before she vomited. Her head split into a million different fragments.

"Cassie, stop. I have your baby. He's fine." She knew that voice. She *dreamed* of that voice.

Cassie trembled violently. No, her mind was playing tricks on her. Van couldn't be here, but her eyes wouldn't focus so she couldn't see who crouched near her. She listened for Samuel.

"My baby. What have you done with my baby?" Cassie croaked out the words and clawed at the ground searching for the rotted-out log where she tried to hide Samuel.

"Cassie! Stop!"

The raised voice shredded her brain into fragments. White spots exploded behind her eyes, and she crumbled to the ground, sobbing through the pain. "Where's my baby?" She couldn't think, repeating the words over and over. They had to tell her. She needed to find Samuel. Warm gentle hands touched her. Cassie curled into a ball covering her head with her arms. Ragged shards of pain sliced through her body.

"He's right here. Hold still, I'm going to roll you over and put him in your arms."

She froze when the words registered. Big hands gently lowered her onto her back, and she felt the weight of her son placed in the crook of her arm. Cassie reached up with her hand and felt him because her eyes remained unfocused. She was unable to see more than a haze of a bundle next to her, but she could hear him. He gurgled and cooed as he moved in her arms. Shaking horribly from sobbing, and from pain, Cassie leaned over and kissed Samuel. She clenched her eyes closed and held back another wave of nausea the movement produced.

"Your uncle isn't going to hurt you anymore."

Cassie's hand stopped stroking her baby at the sound of his voice. Van's voice? No, her mind was playing tricks on her, just like her eyes. "Where is my father?"

"Is there another threat?"

Cassie heard a different voice that time. She blinked hard trying to clear her vision. The sound of a fire crackling somewhere near her acted as a lightning rod, bringing her back to the clearing where her uncle had tried to kill her. He'd taken pleasure in telling her he was going to beat her to death and leave Samuel for the wolves.

"She said something about her father. I wonder where her mother is."

It *had to be* Van's voice, but Cassie knew it couldn't be. She was still dreaming, only this was a different kind of nightmare.

"She's dead," Cassie spoke between shuddering breaths. She could feel the tears falling down her cheeks but did nothing to wipe them away.

"Cassie, the baby needs to eat. Do you have a bottle for him?" Van's disembodied voice asked.

She blinked back the haze and glanced down at her baby, seeing him clearly. Her finger stroked his cheek, and he turned to suckle at the motion. He was wrapped in a big fleece shirt made of a thick warm material, definitely not something she'd had when she fled the mountaintop.

Slowly she rolled her head. Van and Travis crouched next to her. She blinked several times, making sure the men were truly there. "How?" So many questions screamed through her mind, but that was the only one she could voice.

"Guardian sent us up here to relay a message to you. We heard your baby crying last night. I came in search of whoever was up here with an infant.

We were going to check on them and give them our extra supplies. I found you just after your uncle caught up with you."

"Is he dead?" Cassie hoped he was, and she knew that was wrong, but it would mean Samuel was safe.

"No, but Van put a bullet through the bastard's shoulder. He'll never hit another person with that arm again." Travis answered. "We've got him patched up and tied up over there with the horses."

"My father?"

"Is he a threat?" Van's voice pulled her eyes to meet his for an instant. She couldn't hold his gaze. The guilt she carried was too much to bear.

"Cassie? Is your father a threat?"

"I don't know. He told me he wanted me to die."

Samuel began to fuss in earnest. Cassie tried to sit up, wincing from nausea and...oh God, the pain.

"What are you doing?"

Van's voice carried sudden concern. An emotion she hadn't heard or seen since her mother died. "I need to nurse him."

"Do you think that's wise?" Travis's question almost brought a smile to her face.

"Why? Do you have the equipment to nurse him?" Van quipped before Cassie could comment.

Travis looked everywhere but at Cassie as if he was embarrassed at the notion of her breastfeeding her son. "Well, no, but...she's been unconscious."

Samuel's angry cry sent everyone into motion. Van's big body moved behind her as he gently slid her up into an elevated recline against his chest. The gentleness of his touch sent a fresh wave of tears down her cheeks. Cassie reached up to unbutton her shirt, but Van's hands stayed their action.

"Travis, her father may be out there. I need you to take the out position until I relieve you or reinforcements arrive."

"Copy that, Skipper." Travis stood up quickly and headed into the darkness.

In another life, the embarrassment the big man showed might have been funny. But there wasn't anything remotely amusing about her life. Van released her hand, and she unbuttoned her shirt. She attempted to lift Samuel, but a shot of pain raced up her arm when she moved.

"Here, let me help you." Van slid his big hand under Samuel and repositioned him against her breast. The baby rooted around and latched on, suckling as if he hadn't been fed all day. She tried to think of how long it had been since she'd last nursed him...three, maybe four hours? The sun was past the ridge, and it was darkening, but the stars weren't out yet.

Cassie carefully laid her head back against Van's chest, unable to support herself without pain rifling through her neck and head.

"What's his name?" The deep bass of his voice rumbled through his chest where she rested.

"Samuel." Silence filled the area around them. Van had adored his grandfather. He'd told her about the wonderful days he'd spent with Grampa Samuel. When she'd named his son, she wanted a name that had good memories associated with it.

"Am I his father?" Van's large hand cradled the baby to her breast. His thumb stroked Samuel's cheek as he fed.

Cassie closed her eyes. She was dying inside, but she wouldn't corner him into taking care of them. "I'm going to go back to Guardian. I think I know someone who will help me get on my feet. We'll be okay. I'm not asking you for anything." Van stiffened behind her.

"Is he *my* son?"

The words were low, and she tensed. Fear

coiled in her gut. "Yes. I've never been with anyone else."

Van didn't move or speak for several minutes. "You were a virgin." The statement didn't need acknowledgement, but she nodded anyway. His hand shook as he trailed it up her uninjured arm. "I didn't know." He placed his chin against her head and whispered, "Thank you for that gift."

Emotion of every imaginable type flitted one after another across her consciousness as she held her son in her arms and was cradled by the man she loved. The man she'd left. A streak of apprehension disturbed the beginnings of hope. What would that action cost her?

When it was time, Van helped her switch Samuel to her other breast. He nursed for a few minutes before he slowed. Samuel struggled to stay awake, the babe was exhausted. Cassie took him off her breast and closed her shirt while Van held him. He lowered Samuel into her arm. The one that didn't hurt. Cassie's thought process faltered when she tried to figure out how to raise him onto her shoulder and burp him.

"Why didn't you tell me?"

She froze, her eyes darted around her. There was anger in his voice. Cassie *knew* anger. She *knew how to react* to anger. Instantly, she curled in on herself, jolting forward and bracing herself on her injured arm so she could hold Samuel tight with her good arm. She cried out as she collapsed around Samuel. Instinct told her to protect him from the beating she *knew* always followed anger.

"Don't, please! Don't hurt him. He's all I have." Cassie begged as she covered her son with her body. The absolute lack of any other sound except Samuel's cries confused her. Cassie took the chance to glance Van's way. She didn't understand the devastated look she saw.

"What did you live through to react like that?" Van lifted away from her and went to the far side of the fire, giving her space. He sat down and stared at her. "I'm not going to hurt you, Cassie. I would never touch you, or my son, in anger."

Her reaction to his question ripped his guts out. His heart, the woman he loved, lay in the dirt, covering his son, begging him not to hurt their baby. He'd seen reactions like hers before. Prisoners with PTSD who'd been rescued from hostile forces showed the same conditioned fear.

He could only guess what those motherfuckers had done to her. The multitude of bruises that covered her exposed skin told a story. He'd examined her before Travis had reached them. She was covered in bruises, new and old. He'd prayed they had another source, but her reactions since she woke spoke volumes. Rage against the men who'd done this filled him.

His gaze traveled across the distance and met the cold stare of one of the men responsible for Cassie's injuries, both mental and physical. Her *family* had done this to her, the people who were supposed to protect her and care for her.

"What did you have to live through to react to me that way?" The question was rhetorical. He could guess, but he probably needed to hear it in her words. He rose, went to the other side of the fire and sat down, facing her. He was going to make them pay. "I'm not going to hurt you, Cassie. I would never touch you, or my son, in anger."

She sat up and faced away from him. He let her compose herself and quiet the baby...his son. Van fed the fire and warmed an MRE for her.

"I'm sorry."

Her soft words barely reached him. He didn't know how to respond to that. What in the hell was she sorry for? He had so many questions. So much he needed to know. He kept his mouth shut and worked on getting some food into her.

"I can't lift him to burp him."

"I'll do that while you eat." He opened her warmed MRE pouch and poured the contents onto the camp plate along with a piece of pound cake and several crackers with a packet of peanut butter. He moved slowly while he made his way around the fire. She watched him with those big brown eyes, never once looking away. The fear that now haunted her gaze hadn't been there a year ago. She was shy and quiet when he'd met her. Now, she was wounded and lost. He set the plate down, along with a canteen of water. He extended his arm toward her slowly, taking the child and lifting him to his shoulder. He leaned back against a log that Travis had drug over near the fire to sit on when he'd arrived earlier. Van draped the fleece shirt over the little body and tapped his tiny back gently. Samuel snuggled into his neck sucking on his fist. "Am I doing this right?"

Other than doing the shit he witnessed on television and the bumbling around earlier today, Van had zero experience with kids. He didn't want to screw up and break his son.

"You won't hurt him. Rub his back every now and then. It helps to dislodge the gas."

Van glanced down at the little body before his eyes returned to Cassie. She reached out and snagged the canteen, lifting it to her lips, drinking deeply.

"Don't chug the water. You've probably got one hell of a concussion." He hated to stop her, but he needed to make sure she didn't get sick.

She immediately set the canteen down as if it had burned her. "I'm sorry."

Van shook his head. "You've nothing to be sorry about. I just didn't want you to get sick. Eat, but take it slowly. Make sure your stomach and head can handle the food and water."

Cassie looked at him before she reached out for the plate. She lifted the fork and glanced back at him.

"Go ahead, eat." Van kept his voice low as if he was talking to a frightened animal. She ate with one eye on him—as if he was going to take her food away.

Samuel let out a huge burp startling Van into a laugh. He ran his palm over his son's back. "How old is he?"

Cassie stopped with a forkful of food halfway

to her mouth. "Two months...maybe? The moon has been full twice since I had him."

"You don't know what day he was born?"

"No. They wouldn't have told me if I asked."

Cassie waited, but when he didn't speak again, she lifted the spoon and ate some more. He gave her several minutes before he asked, "Why did you stay?"

"It wasn't by choice. I tried to leave after I first came back. My uncle beat me up pretty good when Mom told them I was pregnant. I knew I had to leave then, but Mom wouldn't come with me. I tried to convince her that I could take care of her... there were people who would help us. She didn't believe me. I begged Mom to come with me, but she wouldn't. I had to protect my unborn child, so I left." Cassie glanced down the meadow toward the granite face of the mountain. "Mom followed me. I didn't know. She'd told me she couldn't leave my father. I made it down the face." Cassie looked at the huge granite surface, apparently lost in memories. She sighed and continued, "I was starting across the meadow when I heard her scream. She must have tripped over something. I found her at the base. She lived for about five minutes. My uncle found me with her. I remember a fist…" Cassie set the plate down and moved closer to the fire. "They kept me locked up in the cabin until I was too far along to try to come down. Then after I had him…no one would be stupid enough to take a baby down this mountain without protection." As if to punctuate her statement the sound of a wolf cry, plaintive and eerie, rolled through the meadow.

"And yet, you did." Van continued to rub his son's back.

Cassie gave a single dip to her chin. "Yeah, two nights ago, they…" Her shoulders lifted in a shuddering sigh… "I had to leave. They were going to kill us. The only question was when. At least we had a chance this way."

Van closed his eyes. If they hadn't been sent here, Cassie would be dead and his son…fuck, he opened his eyes again and glared across the clearing at the waste of sperm that had abused his family.

"Why didn't you tell me about him? Did you know before you left me?" He manned up and picked that scab in front of her. His emotions bled out. He could tell she saw the hurt and maybe the loneliness, but he needed to know. He deserved an answer.

"I was with you for three months. I know how you feel about women and families." Cassie glanced at him. Her sad, small voice made no sense whatsoever to him.

"You know how I feel about families? I…I don't understand. We talked a lot, but never about that. Did we?" Van lowered Samuel and tucked him into his arm, holding him like a football. He wrapped the fleece around his arm, making sure to keep his son warm. Warm, dry and fed. Travis's words had echoed around his head all afternoon.

"You talked with your men. When you did, I listened." Cassie shrugged with her good arm. "I couldn't be one of the women you talked about."

"What?" Van was completely lost. What women had they talked about? He searched his brain for any memory of him talking with his men about families. He couldn't remember a single time they'd spoken about…*oh…fuck.* "You heard us giving each other shit, didn't you? Did you think we were serious? We always dog on each other, but Cassie, each one of those men would be over the moon if they found a woman they could love, one that would love them back. And if that woman understood what they did? Every damn one of us would rotate the earth from its axis to keep her.

What you heard was moronic bullshit that we spout to each other to keep us from fixating on the fact that we *don't* have a woman or a family. It's all a farce, a macho pretense."

Cassie stared across the campsite at him. "You didn't."

Van blinked, trying to understand. "I didn't what?"

"You didn't come after me." She lowered her eyes and picked at a hole in her jeans.

"You vanished without a word. I had no idea what was going through your head—or where you had gone. Believe it or not, I was hurt, and I was pissed. When I finally pulled my head out of my ass, I couldn't get anything out of Guardian except that you had completed your contract. Whoever shielded your information did a fucking fantastic job." Van struggled to control the anger he still felt. If he'd been able to find out where she lived, would he have searched her out? Hell, he didn't know... no, fuck that, he'd have tracked her down and demanded to know what he'd done to make her run.

"I told Jewell I'd come back if I felt like I was in danger. I tried. She wanted me to contact her and let her know about the baby. I couldn't. My father hid the ham radio. I had no way of contacting her other than coming down the mountain."

"Jewell?"

"Yes. Jewell King."

A light bulb pinged on. He was starting to get a picture. "She knew you were pregnant?"

Cassie nodded.

"Did she know the baby was mine?"

Cassie nodded again, and Van laughed at his sudden insight. The Kings were notoriously family oriented. There was little doubt in his mind that he and Travis had been pawns in an operation manufactured by Cassie's very powerful friend. When Cassie hadn't made contact, he'd been sent to check up on her. He needed to make sure he sent that woman flowers. Or not. Rumor had it she was married to a former assassin. *Former* assassin... right, no such thing...just like there was no such thing as a former Marine. Van had no doubt the motto for Ms. King's fiancé was, "once an assassin, always an assassin." Maybe a quick phone call and a thank you would suffice.

"Why are you laughing at me?"

Van shook his head at her question. "I'm not. I'm actually marveling at the way things have happened. Come over here." He lifted the arm that wasn't holding his son. At Cassie's hesitance, he smiled at her. "I wanted to find you. I was stonewalled. Every time I tried to get information on where you lived, I was blocked. I lost my shit when you left me, but, you need to know I haven't been with anyone since you. I love you, Cassie. I was going to propose to you in Atlanta. I wanted to a month before we came back, but you deserved better than a twisted wire ring made at a makeshift camp in the mountains of Kashmir."

He witnessed the flash of emotion in her eyes as she lifted them to meet his. Van lowered his arm and adjusted the shirt over Samuel's little body again. "I think Jewell King knew something wasn't right. She split up my team to send me here, to find you. To give you a message."

"What was the message?" Cassie shifted and winced in discomfort.

Van patted the ground next to him. "Please, I promise I'll never touch you in anger, and I'll never let anyone lay a hand on you or our son." Van didn't force the issue. He could only imagine how fragile Cassie's grasp on everything was right now. He barely held back his overwhelming need to hold her close, so no one could ever hurt her again, but his gut told him that she needed to trust him enough to come to him. He couldn't...no, he *wouldn't* make her decisions for her.

Cassie moved, slowly. She lifted to her knees and carefully shuffled over toward him. "What was the message?" She repeated her question as she came closer.

CHAPTER 10

*C*assie longed to feel Van's warmth again. She shuffled on her knees, closer but not close enough that he could swing out and hit her. Although with Samuel in his arms, the danger wasn't hers, it was her son's.

Van glanced down at Samuel again and tucked a small corner of the fleece shirt into the crook of his arm. "Jewell King told me to tell you that she had an assignment for you and I quote, 'The puzzle master is necessary.'"

Cassie sat on her heels. Jewell King told her she was necessary. She blinked, trying to gauge what those words meant, but without context, she was at a loss for how to solve that puzzle. She shot a quick glance at Van before her gaze wandered across the way. Her uncle's eyes fixed on her. Hatred and rage poured off him. "What will happen to him? To us?"

Van glanced at her uncle before he looked down at Samuel. "He will be turned over to the authorities. He'll never hurt you again."

Cassie knew the words should be a relief, but she didn't believe them. Her uncle and her father had scarred her so deeply, she doubted she'd ever forget the pain. She chose not to argue the point because making any comment on what Van said could cause him to be angry. She glanced at Samuel. Her hands itched with the need to hold her son.

"I have a helicopter inbound. They will be here in the morning. First, we are stopping in Buckskin Junction. The local authorities will need to document the abuse you've suffered, and you need to make a report. Then we are going to a safe place. It isn't far by air. We'll stay there until we figure out what we want to do. Where we want to go."

Cassie snapped her attention from her son to Van. "We?"

He glanced down at the sleeping baby. "A man can raise a child with love."

Cassie fell back and winced at the pain the

sudden jarring impact caused. She shook her head, terror lacing its fingers through her entire body. "Please don't take my baby from me." She whispered the plea, afraid to say it out loud.

Van's head snapped up. "Never. I would never take Samuel away from you. I won't force you to make any decisions, Cassie. We'll go as slow as you need, but I'm not giving up on you or my son. I loved you. I still do. No matter how much I told myself to forget you, that you'd played me, I couldn't do it. I couldn't stop wondering what I'd done wrong."

Cassie scooted closer to him. Close enough that he could easily hit her if she made him angry. She strangled her fear and scooted even closer. She could feel his warm body. "I never wanted to leave you. I was afraid for my mom. My uncle said he'd kill her if I didn't come back." Cassie reached out and ran a dirty finger across the shirt that kept her son warm. "I think my uncle killed her anyway. I think he was at the top of the mountain and shoved her off the cliff. I can't prove it." Cassie glanced up quickly, caught Van's eyes and diverted hers immediately. "He said her death was my fault. He called me a murderer."

"Where was your father?" Van shifted slightly,

bringing their arms into contact. Cassie flinched and pulled away.

"He..." She drew as deep of a breath as she could and exhaled it while she stared out into the darkness. "He never stopped my uncle. I don't know if he didn't care or if he just hated me that much. He never hit me, but he never stopped my uncle from beating me, either."

"Cassie?" She turned her attention back to Van. "Did he?" Van shifted and closed his eyes. "Did he rape you?"

Cassie shook her head and refocused on the darkness that surrounded them. "No. There were times I thought he might, but...no." She glanced at Samuel again. "I want him to grow up in a good world. Not this one." She closed her eyes. "I'm so sorry."

"For what?"

"For everything." She opened her eyes and turned toward him, wrapping her good arm around her legs, holding on to the thin material of her jeans she propped her head on her knees as she stared at him. "The decisions I made hurt you. I never meant for that to happen. I believed the things you said to your team. Plus, I knew my mom would be badly hurt or killed if I didn't return. They always took their anger out on her, and sometimes me, but she shielded me from the majority of it. I... I felt like I had no choice but to come back. I knew they wouldn't be pleased I was pregnant, but I never imagined what happened. I actually thought they'd let me go."

They sat in silence for a while longer. Cassie listened to the wolves crying back and forth, but the sound no longer punched spikes of fear through her.

Van shifted Samuel into his other arm and tucked the shirt around his little body. "I think you made decisions based on what you knew to be true. I wish you would have talked to me. Maybe things would have been different, but hindsight is always twenty-twenty. From here on, we have to talk to each other. I have to know what you're thinking and why. I swear on my life that I will never hurt you or Samuel. I'll never let another person raise a hand to you as long as I have breath in my lungs."

"I'd like to believe that, Van." Cassie felt the tears falling and did nothing to hide them.

"I know." His hand reached out slowly. She closed her eyes and tried not to flinch. His finger-tips pushed her hair away from her face. "I'll spend a lifetime proving it to you, if that is what it takes."

Van patted the saddle blankets next to him. "Take Samuel and rest while you can. Travis is watching over us, and I won't sleep until I know you're safe." Cassie looked longingly at the padded ground. She glanced at Samuel and the blankets. "Here, let me help. You lay down and get comfortable, I'll give him to you when you're ready."

Van moved away from the blankets giving Cassie the confidence to move toward them. She carefully lowered herself to the ground and accepted Samuel when Van lowered him.

"I'm here, and you're safe." Van's finger traced Samuel's face before his gaze slid to Cassie. "I promise."

CHAPTER 11

*T*ravis never asked to be relieved, and Van appreciated the gesture. They checked in occasionally, a few quiet words between warriors. Van checked on Cassie's uncle numerous times, making sure the son of a bitch's hands were bound and that he hadn't somehow managed to loosen the rope.

The sun was starting to crest the last time he left Cassie and Samuel and headed over to check on the uncle. The older man's eyes lifted heavenward at the distant whop of a copter's approach.

A sneer spread across Van's face. "Oh, that's not for you. That's for us. You get to go down the mountain on horseback with the local police. I'm

119

sure they will give you something for the pain...eventually."

The man rolled his eyes toward Van. "She's evil. She sees answers in puzzles that don't exist. She killed her mother. When I tell the authorities, she'll be behind bars. Not me."

"The assault I witnessed, the marks and bruises all over her body, those things will put you away for a good long time."

"I don't know what you think you saw, but I never hit that girl."

"Right, and the clear impression on her ribs of the boot you're wearing is just decoration?"

The older man's eyes narrowed, and he snapped his mouth shut. The helicopter cleared the mountains, and Van smiled. He'd never been so happy to see a shiny black gunship bearing his company's logo. He shook his head. Damn, he wondered how the bosses got approval for a privately-owned UH-60A Black Hawk, although the upgrades he could see were considerable. He yanked on the old man's ropes one more time and headed back across the clearing.

Cassie was awake, nursing Samuel. She squinted at the helicopter as it neared. Van saw Travis exit the woods and head toward their prisoner. Van grabbed one of the shirts that he'd used as a blanket for Cassie last night and approached her. "Things are going to get windy and noisy. Let me drape this over you?" He held up the shirt, having to yell the last portion of his request.

She nodded and curved over their son in a protective pose. He draped the shirt over them and quickly and efficiently tucked it under her legs. He could feel her flinch at his touch and damned the man across the clearing again.

He could hear Samuel crying as the helicopter set down close to the face of the mountain, but far enough out into the large meadow to allow the blades to rotate without issue. The pilots remained with the aircraft, but five others spilled out.

He watched as they crouched and ran toward where he stood. He recognized Isiah Reichs and Sampson Waters. The badge and uniform of the third man explained his presence. Van turned his attention to the other two. One carried a black bag and wore an eye patch and the other, well, the other looked like a walking mountain.

"Wheeler?" The man with the bag stuck out his hand. "Doctor Adam Cassidy. I understand Ms. Valentine is in need of some attention?"

Van nodded and shook the man's hand. He

glanced back over his shoulder but held the doctor before he could head her direction. "Doc, she's been physically abused for a long time. She might not let you look at her."

The doctor's face steeled, and he nodded. "Unfortunately, I've dealt with these types of cases before. Let me see if I can get her to let me take a look." He shouldered past Van and headed to where Cassie sat with his shirt draped around her shoulders.

Van turned his attention to the man in front of him.

"I'm Jason King." The massive man extended his hand toward Van. *Oh shit. The boss.* The top of the heap. He had at least three levels of command between him and the man standing in front of him.

"Sir." Van shook his hand.

"I need a SitRep. Imagine my surprise when I'm talking with my people and hear an emergency broadcast from a team I didn't know was deployed to Montana." The big guy crossed his arms over his chest and looked down at Van.

"Sir, I was directed here. Orders from Starling and Jewell King." Van couldn't keep his gaze from wandering to where the doctor sat talking to Cassie.

"My sister sent you out here? Why?" The gravelly voice refocused Van's attention on Jason King.

"To find Cassie, give her a message, and bring her out." Van gestured toward where Doctor Cassidy was holding his son. Thankfully, it seemed Cassie was cooperating.

"You have a previous acquaintance with Ms. Valentine if my memory serves correctly."

Van dipped his head in acknowledgment. Jason King took off his glasses and pinched the bridge of his nose for a few moments. "The child is...?"

Van turned and faced the CEO of Guardian International. "He's my son. I didn't know she was pregnant. She came back to take care of her mom." Van wasn't willing to tell any more of Cassie's story without her permission.

"And I take it my sister had some type of knowledge of this situation?"

Van nodded as his gaze swung to the far side of the pasture. Cassie's uncle was up on his feet, handcuffed and sandwiched between Sampson and the local sheriff they'd coptered in. Reichs and Travis were talking as they followed.

"Mr. King, I'll be taking this one down with me. Sampson will ride shotgun. I appreciate the ride up." The sheriff turned to Van. "We'll need to talk to Ms. Valentine when she's able. Guardian has requested we hold her uncle until they determine jurisdiction." The sheriff shook his head. "Not sure why there are any jurisdiction issues, but we'll hold him until we get clarification." He motioned towards Sampson who fell into step heading toward the horses.

Isiah Reichs stood next to Jason King and crossed his arms over his chest. The two could have been molded out of the same clay. Van glanced over his shoulder again. "Sir? Do you mind?"

Jason nodded his approval, and Van double-timed it back to where Cassie cowered watching the doctor examine Samuel.

"Oh, he is a happy baby, isn't he?" Doctor Cassidy put his stethoscope away as he spoke. "He'll need to have his inoculations, and I'd love to get measurements so we can monitor his growth, but overall, he looks healthy, if a little underweight."

"I tried." Cassie's voice rang with fear as she offered her apology. Damn it, Van wouldn't let her be traumatized any further. He slowed his approach as he drew closer.

"I'm sure you did, but when momma doesn't get

proper nutrition, the baby doesn't either. You did nothing wrong. Now, can I take a look at that arm?"

Cassie cradled her injured arm against her stomach and shook. She radiated fear. Van crouched down near her, not close enough to scare her. "Doc, would you happen to know of any women in the local area who could do the examination?"

Cassie's eyes swung up to him, her thanks clearly written in her expression.

"As a matter of fact, I do. I was told we were going to be heading straight back to the complex in South Dakota. We have a female doctor on staff. Her name is Ember, and she a a fantastic physician."

Van took the baby from the doctor and sat down beside Cassie. He lowered his voice. "Maybe just let him look at your arm? The helicopter ride will be jarring. I'll be right here. I've got Samuel, and I promise, nobody will hurt either of you."

Cassie glanced at him from under her eyelashes and then looked at the doctor. It took several long moments before she nodded in agreement. Van paced near where the doctor examined her, lightly bouncing Samuel as he moved. Cassie's eyes tracked them. He smiled and winked at her. Her eyes widened, her face flushed red, and she lowered her eyes shyly. Van turned and hid a smile. That expression was the gold he'd been digging for. There was hope.

CHAPTER 12

*C*assie sat on the long wrap around porch of the bed and breakfast in Buckskin Junction. Four months had gone by since Van had rescued her and Samuel from certain death—four months of living a dream. Van had never once left her side. He'd taken a leave of absence from Guardian, and they'd grown closer. Cassie had held herself back. She had needed to close the nightmare chapters of her past before she could allow herself to move forward with Van.

She rocked on the porch and watched through hanging baskets of pink flowers as he walked from the diner back toward the bed and breakfast. They were waiting to hear the verdict of the trial. Both her father and uncle had been arrested. Her uncle for attempted murder, felonious assault, and kidnapping. Her father as an accomplice to all of her uncle's crimes. They couldn't prove her uncle had anything to do with her mother's death, but there was no statute of limitations on murder. She'd testified for two days and endured the public defender's attempts to paint her as the villain.

To say it had been an ordeal would have been an understatement. She left the courthouse this afternoon feeling like an exposed nerve. Everything hurt. Physically, she'd been ill both before and after testifying. Mentally, she'd been pushed to her emotional breaking point as both the defense and the prosecutor made her recount the events of the year she was held by her family. The pictures taken of her injuries after Van rescued her were shown in vivid detail. She'd lived through the shame of her decisions over and over. She'd cried until she couldn't, but she never once asked for a break. She never once told a lie and she never once stopped counting on Van for support.

His testimony was the last of the trial. The prosecution said his credentials and the reputation of his agency were the golden nails in her family's coffin. She agreed. Van was clear, professional and wielded his agency's authority like a weapon.

When he was dismissed from the witness stand, he walked straight to her, extended his hand and they left the courtroom.

She smiled at the small Styrofoam container he held up and waggled. He'd been extolling the virtues of the banana cream pie since they turned west out of Butte. He dropped into the rocking chair next to her and held out a plastic fork before he popped the top and groaned. "Oh, yes."

Cassie dipped the fork through the creamy filling. It was as good as he'd said. She leaned back in the chair and closed her eyes, enjoying the quiet with Van. Samuel was safe with Jewell and her new husband. Her friend had flown out to see her within days of her being brought down from the mountain. Jewell had been a steadfast and semi-permanent fixture in their lives since then.

Van cleared his throat and took a deep breath. "I got a call from the District Attorney's office while I was at the diner. The jury lost no time in returning a verdict." She stopped rocking and gave him her undivided attention. "Your uncle was found guilty of first-degree attempted murder, aggravated assault and aggravated kidnapping. He'll spend the rest of his life in the Montana State Prison. Your father was found guilty of accessory to first-degree attempted murder, and aggravated kidnapping and sentenced to fifty-years in the state prison. He'll be a very old man before he gets out." His eyes held hers until she looked away, closed her eyes and rested her head on the back of the rocker.

Silence settled around them and she was shocked to realize she felt very little emotion at hearing the fate of her uncle and father. They no longer had any power to hurt her.

"Hey...are you going to be okay?" Van's soft baritone caressed her senses.

She smiled faintly and opened her eyes, rolling her head toward him. "As much as I want to say I hated having to relive those days, it...I don't know...it was like telling the judge and jury what happened released the power my uncle and my father had over me. Does that make sense?"

Van nodded and licked the fork he was holding. "It was cathartic."

Cassie glanced at him, and he shrugged. "That means cleansing. You were able to wring it out of your system."

"Cathartic." Cassie nodded her head. Yeah, that was a word she would remember. She reached out and intertwined her fingers with his. Van glanced over and smiled. He'd never pushed her for more. He accepted what she could give when she could give it, and he was the best daddy to Samuel. Cassie kept waiting for the bough to break, but he proved to her day in and day out that he adored his son. He also proved he loved her in countless little ways, like the flowers or small treats and trinkets he'd bring back with him after periodic meetings he still had with Guardian. He'd pitch in doing laundry, cooking or dishes. Laughter and happiness replaced the fear and loneliness in which she used to exist. Van never raised his voice or snapped when she'd ask questions. His eyes held his love for her, and she witnessed it every time she looked at him.

She tugged on his hand bringing his eyes back to her. "I love you."

He smiled and leaned over for a kiss. "I love you, too." He let her initiate the kiss, let her determine when to pull away. It was always like that with him. He never assumed. He always let her lead at her pace.

Cassie stood still holding his hand. "I think it's time."

Van looked at his watch, a scowl pushed his brows together. "For what?"

"For you to make love to me." She studied his reaction of shock and then concern.

"You don't have to do this. We have all the time in the world." He still held her hand and gazed into her eyes.

"I know, but I want to." Cassie tugged lightly on his hand. He stood and followed her up to her bedroom. He'd booked a separate one for himself. Always the gentleman.

He closed the door behind him but didn't come toward her. "Cassie, I wasn't expecting this. I don't have any birth control with me."

"But I do." She went to the bed and pulled down the covers before she turned and started to unbutton her shirt. "I'm on the pill. I have been since my exam after..."

Van watched her as she disrobed. He held at the door, yet she could see the desire in his eyes when he looked at her. Cassie dropped the last of her clothes and walked forward, unbuttoning his shirt and pulling the tail out of his jeans. She pushed his shirt over his shoulders and kissed a crescent-shaped scar she found there. He shrugged the shirt off and continued to watch her as if he were enthralled. She undid his belt buckle, unhooked his button and lowered his zipper. Slowly she pushed his jeans and boxers down his hips, over his ass and freed his erection. She took his cock in her hand, and that seemed to break the spell. Van slowly slipped his arms around her and brought her to his chest.

"You have to promise me you'll tell me if I do anything that scares you." He lowered and kissed her, taking the lead for the first time since he'd rescued her.

Cassie breathed a sigh of relief. This was how she longed for things to be. She trusted Van. She always had, but the abuse had clouded that trust. Not his fault, or hers, yet it was an issue she'd had to work through. Van suddenly chuckled against her lips. She pulled away and blinked up at him in surprise.

"You've got me hobbled." He shot his eyes to his feet. His jeans pooled around his cowboy boots. Cassie started giggling and then laughed. She backed up and sat on the bed while he did a dance getting his boots off without falling on his face. He stepped out of his jeans and flicked off his socks before coming for her. The smile on her face broadened as she backed up onto the middle of the bed.

Van soon hovered over her. His smile was as wide as hers. "You make me happy."

His words found another dark spot in her heart and illuminated it with warmth and love. She reached up to him and pulled him down on top of her. She wanted to feel his weight. She needed to feel secure and protected and being held in his arms while they made love was the haven she remembered when the nights were hopeless. Cassie lost herself in his kiss.

His hands made slow, torturous paths across her skin. His lips followed, and Cassie let herself drown in the sensation of his skin against hers. He licked, kissed and touched every inch of her skin, driving her to a level of need she hadn't realized she was capable of reaching. He lifted up and centered himself between her legs. He closed his eyes and swallowed before he asked, "Are you sure?"

She could see what it cost him to stop and ask. The strain of his muscles sent a vibration through him, but he opened his eyes and looked down at her, and she knew, without a shadow of a doubt— she was sure. The love that radiated from him was as real as the touch of his hands. "I'm sure."

He closed his eyes and slowly, carefully, moved

forward breaching her, making them one. She grasped him tightly and held him to her.

"I love you."

His words acted as a key that unlocked the explosion building within. Her body clenched tight, and she rocked against his thrusts, taking her own pleasure. He buried his face against her neck and groaned as he thrust through his own release.

Cassie held him while they both calmed. She relaxed in the glow of their intimacy. Van rolled them to their sides, so they were facing each other. He pushed her hair back out of her face, and she ran her fingers through his beard. He smiled and caught her hand, kissing each finger. He leaned up on his elbow and looked down at her. His finger traced her jawline. "When you're ready, I want to marry you."

"Is that a proposal?" Cassie searched his eyes as they smiled down at her.

"No, our love, our family, and our lives aren't a proposal to me. They are our destiny."

The End

For Now

Keep reading for a sneak peek at Jacob, The Kings of Guardian - Book One!

*C*urled on the crude bench, Tori blinked and fought to keep her focus. She etched one more line into the soft plaster of her cell wall. The added line brought the total to sixty-seven white marks scratched into the dirty plaster. Her mind twisted, muddled by fragmented thoughts. The words that haunted her formed a familiar cadence. *When would they come? When would the pain stop? Is it morning or evening? Will I die today?*

A door slammed at the far end of the corridor, and the echo lingered in the cell. A low rumble of male voices reached her. She recognized the familiar tones. The guards. They no longer cared if she overheard them.

Terror spiked through her. *Please, God, let it be*

morning! Which guard remained? Was it Emad, the day guard, who slept at the desk at the end of the hall and moved only when someone knocked at the door, or Kassar, the night guard, evil incarnate? An uncontrollable shiver rattled Tori's body. Just like Pavlov's damn dogs, her body reacted to the sound of Kassar's voice. Now just the thought of him induced the response.

Kassar had held her head under water while another guard pressed glowing coals from a hand-rolled cigarette into the soles of her feet. The smoldering cinders seared through the ulcerated abscesses already branded deep into her arches from torture on previous nights.

Her screams pressed oxygen from her lungs. Desperate for air, her body inhaled the vile sludge that passed as water, while Kassar held her head under the surface. A vicious grab of her hair pulled her up, choking and vomiting. The bastard made sure she remained conscious. Kassar knew how to maximize the anguish and terror he inflicted.

"What is your mission?" His guttural English demanded an answer.

"I'm a photographer!" Her head was immediately plunged back into the putrid fluid sloshing in the bucket. Again searing agony ripped across the sole of

her foot, and again the excruciating pain forced an involuntary scream and inhale. Just before she blacked out, hands grabbed her hair and pulled her to the surface.

"American whore! Tell me who sent you!"

"Photographer, freelance... nobody! Please! Let me go!" Her cries of innocence had only inflamed his anger.

The interrogations and torture had not broken her. Her captors knew only her cover story. That she maintained her cover story signed her death certificate just as certainly as admitting she worked for the CIA. *No one will help. I know it.* The freelance photography company would be a dead-end. Rightfully, no one there would claim knowledge of her. The CIA would never have the opportunity to confirm or deny her employment; she'd never confessed to working for them. There would be no ransom, no happy-ever-after ending to this nightmare. Death at Kassar's hand would be the only escape.

Her abused body curled inward, longing for a warmth vaguely remembered. A distant rattle of the guard's keys being thrown on the desk indicated whoever watched over her had stirred. Had Emad provided water or food? Would this be another day of starvation and thirst?

She lifted her head from the bench and attempted to sit, biting her fist against the nausea her movement caused. Tori panted and waited for the violent lurch of the room to stop. At some point, a crude wooden bucket had appeared inside the door of her cell. The mere thought of food or water drove her aching body into action. She put weight on her good leg, holding her useless arm close, and stood cautiously. The effort it took to cross the tiny cell had become a gauntlet of pain and determination. The sores and blisters on her feet cracked open and bloody footprints marked her progress. Yet starvation made one hell of a motivator, even for those who knew their fate.

Please, God, please let there be food. Her pitiful approach startled a rat the size of a small dog away from the bucket. He squeaked his displeasure at the interruption and slid his lean body through the bars of the cell door. A small piece of bread and something that almost resembled broth lay at the bottom of the rotted wooden vessel. *Thank you, sweet Jesus!*

Tori pulled the container toward her. An echo of the scrape of wood on stone lingered in the silence of the cell. The putrid smell from the fetid congealed slime at the bottom rolled up to her. She gagged and tried to hold in the sound of her dry heaves. *No wonder the rat left without a fight.*

Heavy steps echoed down the hallway toward her. The noise of the bucket or her retches must have caught the guard's attention. Tori shoved the gelatinous hunk of bread into her mouth and chewed. The familiar pop of pellet-like substances provided indisputable proof maggots infested the bread. She pressed her hand against her mouth, forcing herself not to regurgitate the only food she had consumed in days. Hysteria fought for control of her tenuous grasp on reality. The sound of footsteps grew louder. She limped away from the iron bars and pressed against the wooden bench that served as the singular piece of furniture in the cell.

Kassar, the evening guard, leered through the bars. Emad stood behind him. Fear gripped her, freezing her muscles, numbing her mind and mentally she started to slip away. The mandatory training classes she'd attended called the phenomena dissociative mental ordering. Tori didn't know when or how she'd first begun to do it, but sometimes when they came to question and beat her, she left... mentally. Usually, the curtain of oblivion fell only for the duration of the attack, but more and more, she lingered in the blackouts that protected her tenuous grasp on reality.

"The whore is useless to us! She is not what they said." Emad spat at her through the bars.

"If she is of no political value and no one claims her, the Elders will give her to me. She begs for mercy now. By the time I've finished with her she will beg for death," Kassar responded and glared at her.

Emad's voice trailed him as he turned and walked away. "You have been warned, Kassar. The Westerners value their women. Do not defile her against the Elders' decrees. The payment will decrease."

"The Elders are fools. She is a filthy infidel! An American—our avowed enemy!" The hatred in his eyes nailed Tori to the wall. Kassar could kill her with one hand. She almost hoped he would. Spittle flew from Kassar's mouth as he switched languages and spoke in heavily accented English. "No pay for a whore. They give you to me soon. I have until you die. Your body food for animals."

"Kassar, you are to obey the Elders' commands for the woman! Do not defile her or kill her. Have your fun tonight. Be useful and make her talk. Your reward will be more than this whore." Emad's sharp reprimand in Kassar's native Afghani dialect earned her a snarl and an evil glare.

Tori understood enough of their language to know her captor's patience neared exhaustion. The guards' exchange left no room for doubt—or hope. Left alone, she turned, inch by excruciating inch, to face the wall, and stared at the display of white marks. Sixty-seven days existing in a hell where her only defense consisted of desperate prayers for the impossible. *How would her father and sister react to her death? Oh God... would they ever know?* She couldn't afford the flood of emotion that threatened to break her. No, she had to bury it all to protect them and herself.

The door at the end of the hall slammed shut. Once again, footsteps echoed menacingly down the hall. So it begins... again. Tori knew she reeked of weakness and fear. Kassar opened the bars and walked toward her. He grabbed her by the neck, lifting her away from the wall, and backhanded her. The force bounced her head off the concrete wall. She slumped against the wooden bench, numb. He untied the string around his *shalwar*, the Afghani version of pants.

"No longer will you hide under the protection of weak old men, American whore. I have watched and waited. I take you tonight. They will not know about tonight or any night after this. Nobody ever returns to the stench of the cells at night." He pulled viciously at the waistband of her garb and moved over her. She didn't resist the blessed darkness that pulled her past the white-hot shards of pain.

Jacob palmed his Interceptor 911. The fourteen inches of sharp-as-shit blade flew silently through the air toward the Afghani guard. The man dropped the person he was assaulting. The muscles in his back convulsed and with frantic movements, the guard reached around, pawing at his back. *Shit.* His knife had missed the guard's heart, but the jailor's sudden movement to the right had merely forestalled his inevitable death. In two quick strides, Jacob corrected his rare error and eliminated the threat. Simple applied torque and force plus acceleration broke the man's neck instantly. The guard's body dropped to the cell floor with a muffled thud. Jacob snatched his knife from the dead body, wiped the bloody blade on the man's clothes, and then signed instructions to his men in the corridor.

They'd eliminated their primary targets soundlessly and efficiently. Pictures and fingerprints had been taken as proof to confirm mission completion for the agency that sanctioned the hits. While his men worked the IDs, Jacob had searched the adjacent room someone had turned into an office.

If he hadn't looked through the paperwork, he never would've realized an American fought for their life in the cell across the compound. Chance, happenstance, destiny or PFL, pure fucking luck—whatever the reasons—he *had* checked. The mission wasn't supposed to be a rescue, but he'd be damned if he'd leave an American. *Damned?* He snorted at his word choice. Yeah right, in his line of work and with his past? His damnation had been signed and sealed—a first-class ticket to hell with Lucifer himself opening the door—but leaving an American prisoner? Not an option. Surprisingly, he still had standards.

While his men searched and cleared the interior of the holding facility with efficient, silent skill, Jacob moved to complete a quick visual assessment of the captive. *Oh, fuck. The prisoner was a woman. Fuck!* Training centered him on the task at hand. Alive. Head trauma and right eye swelling. Her left arm hung awkwardly—a break or a dislocated shoulder. One distinguishable black hematoma on her leg indicated a possible closed fracture. Deeply-caked grime covered her body and probably obscured more injuries. The vivid and extensive bruises over her body told the story of continuous beatings, but visually he'd be hard pressed to distinguish the bruises from the thick layer of muck that covered her. His glance landed on her feet. *The bastards!* He'd seen men tortured to this degree, but never had he seen such brutality inflicted on a woman. A glance at the wall displayed the etched lines in the soft plaster. A record of her days? *"A" for effort, "F" for accuracy.* According to the documents he seized, there weren't nearly enough marks.

He tried not to compound her injuries when he lifted her and silently cursed. Too damn easy to lift. Just skin and bones. Far too light for her obvious height. She probably wouldn't survive the trip to the aircraft. Hatred for her captors pumped through his veins as certainly as the blood that kept him alive. Within three strides into the corridor, Jacob's team closed ranks and formed a protective shield around him. When the team cleared the building, Jacob took his first deep breath since he'd walked into the holding facility less than four minutes ago. The rancid stench below had violated his senses. Outside, the team kept to the shadows, and with speed born from many operations, they cleared the compound. Jacob assessed the uneven ground, jutting rock abutments, and drought-stricken bushes. The rugged terrain that surrounded the camp would slow the team's egress.

"Skipper, we've got five clicks to the extraction point. You need me to carry her?"

Jacob glared at Chief, his communications specialist, as they continued to maneuver through the craggy hills using the natural valleys and shrub as cover. Jacob's size and physical condition allowed him to carry the woman without effort even across the rocky and unforgiving terrain. His middle finger threw a 'fuck you' at the massive man. "Take the point and signal the bird we are en route." The big man flashed a rare grin and sprinted forward.

His five-man team functioned better than any proverbial well-oiled machine. All parts worked as one. The squad knew the job at hand and performed it with precise, calculated efficiency.

Breaking down? Not an option. Each man provided essential skills. As experts in their fields, they were handpicked for the honor of being on Alpha team. Elite warriors. Honed and perfected in the art of war. The men were equal parts of the whole, and each would likely burn in the same pit in hell when the grim reaper caught up with them.

Jacob's eyes never stopped scanning the horizon, his peripheral vision alert to any movement as he pushed his team forward. The safety of his men and concentration on the extraction point focused his attention to the end of the basin.

Jacob felt her head rock toward him. He glanced down again and looked into dark blue eyes that didn't seem to focus. He watched her pass out again. Thank God. He didn't need a screaming or crying woman on his hands. He didn't do female tears. Ever. That really had to be in his job description somewhere.

Tori felt a soft touch on her face and heard the drawl of a deep baritone. "Honey, we have to put your shoulder back in the socket." Opening her eye, she turned toward the soothing voice and tried to focus. His eyes were almost a steel color. He had a handsome face, strong chin, and cheekbones. His nose had been broken once or twice, but the irregularity added to his rugged handsomeness. She noticed his thick black hair fell long against his collar, longer than Tori knew a military man's hair should be. Oh... okay... she was hallucinating. It had to be because there was no other explanation if he wasn't military. She reached out and touched his face. Her hand shook as she felt his warm skin. "Are you real?"

In an instant, his solemn face changed as he smiled at her. "Yeah, honey, I'm real. You're on your way home. Doc here needs to set your shoulder. I'm not going to lie to you. It's going to hurt like hell."

Her eyes never left his. "Who?"

"Consider me your guardian angel."

ALSO BY KRIS MICHAELS

Kings of the Guardian Series

Jacob: Kings of the Guardian Book 1

Joseph: Kings of the Guardian Book 2

Adam: Kings of the Guardian Book 3

Jason: Kings of the Guardian Book 4

Jared: Kings of the Guardian Book 5

Jasmine: Kings of the Guardian Book 6

Chief: The Kings of Guardian Book 7

Jewell: Kings of the Guardian Book 8

Jade: Kings of the Guardian Book 9

Justin: Kings of the Guardian Book 10

Christmas with the Kings

Drake: Kings of the Guardian Book 11

Dixon: Kings of the Guardian Book 12

Passages: The Kings of Guardian Book 13

Promises: The Kings of Guardian Book 14

A Backwater Blessing: A Kings of Guardian Crossover Novella

Montana Guardian: A Kings of Guardian Novella

Guardian Defenders Series

Gabriel

Maliki

John

Jeremiah

Guardian Security Shadow World

Anubis (Guardian Shadow World Book 1)

Asp (Guardian Shadow World Book 2)

Lycos (Guardian Shadow World Book 3)

Thanatos (Guardian Shadow World Book 4)

Tempest (Guardian Shadow World Book 5)

Smoke (Guardian Shadow World Book 6)

Reaper (Guardian Shadow World Book 7)

Hope City

Hope City - Brock

HOPE CITY - Brody- Book 3

Hope City - Ryker - Book 5

Hope City - Killian - Book 8

STAND ALONE NOVELS

SEAL Forever - Silver SEALs

A Heart's Desire - Stand Alone

Hot SEAL, Single Malt (SEALs in Paradise)

Hot SEAL, Savannah Nights (SEALs in Paradise)

ABOUT THE AUTHOR

USA Today and Amazon Bestselling Author, Kris Michaels is the alter ego of a happily married wife and mother. She writes romance, usually with characters from military and law enforcement backgrounds.

Made in the USA
Coppell, TX
27 June 2024

34003407R00089